THE VIKING

saga four

Hammer of the Gods

THE VIKING

saga four

Hammer
of the Gods

Christopher Tebbetts

PUFFIN BOOKS

PUFFIN BOOKS
Published by Penguin Group
Penguin Young Readers Group,
345 Hudson Street, New York, New York 10014, U.S.A.
Penguin Books Ltd, 80 Strand, London WC2R ORL, England
Penguin Books Australia Ltd, 250 Camberwell Road, Camberwell, Victoria 3124, Australia
Penguin Books Canada Ltd, 10 Alcorn Avenue, Toronto, Ontario, Canada M4V 3B2
Penguin Books (N.Z.) Ltd, 182-190 Wairau Road, Auckland 10, New Zealand

Published by Puffin Books, a division of Penguin Young Readers Group, 2003

1 3 5 7 9 10 8 6 4 2

Text copyright © 17th Street Productions,
an Alloy company, 2003
All rights reserved
Book design by Jim Hoover
The text of this book is set in Arrus BT

ISBN 0-14-250032-1

Printed in the United States of America

For Ilse and Cy

CHAPTER ONE

What if she's dead? What if Erik the Horrible already got what he wanted and Asleif is expendable? What if . . .

It had been nothing but "what if" for Zack Gilman since coming home from the ninth century for the third time. He sat at the workbench in his room with his head down, asking himself the same questions over and over.

What if I can't get back there? What if I do, but it's too late?

Of course, what did "too late" mean? Technically, everything in the Viking world had all happened over a thousand years ago. But the question wasn't how much time had passed. The question was whether or not Yggdrasil's Key would bring him back soon enough, and far back in time enough, to keep something horrible from happening to Asleif.

Zack absently fingered the rusted three-pronged key that hung on a length of cord around his neck. He had learned a lot about the key since that day he literally stumbled across it in the Metrodome parking lot. But he had never figured out how to predict when the key would shuttle him back and forth between the two worlds.

The last time, it had literally plucked him out of the air and dropped him back home again. Zack replayed the scene in his head. Could he have done anything to save Asleif? He

1

saw her face, eyes wide but no emotion on her features as Erik the Horrible pressed a long knife to her cheek. Erik wanted the key, and Zack would have given it to him, too, to save Asleif's life. But Jok, and the other Vikings of Zack's tribe, had stopped him from doing it. They had tackled him off the edge of a cliff, and as they all fell toward the water below, the key had begun to pull Zack through time. Instead of falling into the water, Zack had landed on his own front lawn, twelve hundred years later.

No matter how many times he replayed the scene in his head, he came to the same conclusion. It had been beyond his control. But it hadn't been beyond Jok's control. Zack knew that Jok valued the quest above everything, including human life. But it was a bitter realization to see just how true that was.

All he could hope for now was to make things right again. But how?

Think, Gilman, think.

A roar came from the other side of Zack's bedroom wall. Then something big slammed against it, sending a shower of books to the floor. *The Vikings. Norse Mythology. The World of the Longships.* They lay in a heap on top of a pile of dirty laundry. Most of them were overdue library books. None had given him a single clue about the quest.

Another slam on the wall brought the bookshelf itself down. Zack rolled his eyes but didn't bother to pick anything up. Best to wait until his father's friends had gone home.

The only corner of the room that wasn't a mess was

Zack's bedside table, where a framed picture of his mother stood. Winnifred Gilman had died when Zack was five. She smiled out at the room now, captured forever with her wild mane of frizzy hair tamed by a purple Minnesota Twins baseball cap. Zack looked over at the photo and wondered what she would have made of all this. Not the quest, but the wild scene in the living room.

She probably would have loved it.

Winnifred Gilman had been a football fan, just like her husband.

Zack could hear Jock now, above everyone else, screaming with pleasure in the living room. Zack was used to the noise, but the idea of a two-hundred-pound Minnesota Vikings superfan coming through the wall was enough to break his usual concentration. Besides, it was the playoffs. That meant buffalo wings, nachos, and jalapeño poppers . . . instead of the usual pretzels, chips, and bean dip.

Zack's stomach rumbled a familiar low growl. His appetite was the one thing that hadn't changed in the last month. And good food in this house was an endangered species.

He hastily scooped up the collection of notes and hand-drawn maps spread out on his workbench and stashed them in a pile of newspapers where they wouldn't be seen.

Opening the door to the hallway was like popping the hatch of a 747 at thirty thousand feet. Everything Zack had been hearing through the walls roared up to full volume.

The blaring television was only the background. The real

noise came from Jock Gilman and his friends, who were now singing at the tops of their considerable lungs.

> *"Purple Pride is coming through*
> *Coming to town and*
> *Coming to get you!*
> *Purple Pride is the way of the game*
> *Of glory, of fame,*
> *The Viking name!"*

As he approached the living room, Zack heard the slapping of high fives and the grunts of a group belly bump.

"HEY! IT'S THE ZACK!" His father came over to throw a sausagelike arm around Zack's neck.

"Where have you been?" Jock asked, sending a cloud of nacho cheese breath in Zack's face. "You did all this work and now you're missing the best part."

Jock had compelled Zack and his sister Valerie to help him decorate the living room that morning. They pushed all the furniture against the wall and threw out the newspapers, magazines, pizza boxes, and junk mail that usually littered the house. Thick strips of masking tape ran across the gold living-room carpet, with "50," "40," "30," "20," and "10" spelled out in more tape, leading toward the fireplace. Over the mantel, a fake goalpost was mounted on the wall, with a TOUCHDOWN! sign suspended between its two cardboard uprights. Torn purple and yellow streamers hung in shreds from the ceiling.

Jock's best friend, Swan Swanson, called out to Zack. "Little Jock!"

All the guys raised and lowered their arms one after the other, greeting Zack with a miniature stadium wave. They were all dressed for the playoffs. Harlan Gustafson and Larry Teegarden wore purple football jerseys and Helga helmets—plastic Viking headgear with white horns on top and blond braids hanging down. Smitty's face was painted purple on one side and gold on the other. His Minnesota sweatshirt was wet down the front, either with sweat or soda, or both.

"Here you go, Zack!" Harlan tossed him an open can of root beer, which slipped through Zack's fingers. The soda fizzed out onto the carpet.

"That's why Zack's quarterback material, not a wide receiver!" Jock said, squeezing Zack's biceps. "He's got a natural throwing arm." Zack pulled away and picked up the soda can.

"Hey, Harlan," crowed Larry. "Next time, think about *not* opening the can before you throw it."

"Don't worry about it," Jock said. He stripped off his XXXL sweatshirt, dropped it onto the puddle of soda, and stepped on it.

"Dad!"

Valerie Gilman, Zack's sixteen-year-old sister, stood glaring in the kitchen door. "That's going to leave a big stain," she said.

"It's all right," Jok said with a shrug. "I've got plenty of sweatshirts." He scratched his bare stomach where a purple

5

MV was painted on either side of his belly button. Valerie rolled her eyes and went back into the kitchen.

For Zack, everyone in the house was a reminder of how much he wanted to get back to the ninth century. Each face was the same as someone he knew in that other world. Jok's daughter Valdis was just as tall and bossy as Valerie Gilman, and usually wore the same sullen expression. His father had the same red beard and huge stature as Jok of Lykill. But of all the pairs of "doubles," Jock and Jok seemed most different. When it mattered, Jok knew how to be take things seriously, but Jock's life was all about football and hoagies.

Of course, since Zack had returned from the ninth century this time he felt like the way he saw the two men was completely turned around. How could he respect Jok the same way after seeing him abandon Asleif like that?

At first the whole parallel universes thing had seemed like a weird joke. Now Zack knew better. It was still weird, but it was no joke. Whatever he felt about Jok now, Zack had also come back more convinced than ever that there was a traitor in Jok's tribe. Even more unsettling, he suspected that the traitor was one of the people closest to Jok, maybe even a member of the tribe's inner council. Zack looked at the faces of the men hanging out in his living room.

Smitty sat and watched the game without speaking. That wasn't unusual. Like his Viking double Sigurd, Smitty was about as talkative as a giraffe. Zack realized he had been staring at him when Smitty let out an enormous, five-second-long belch that popped his thought bubble. All the other guys cracked up. After football, passing gas seemed to be their favorite pastime.

"Good one, Smitty," said Swan.

Zack grabbed the last handful of nachos. "How far along is the game?" It was easier than asking how much longer he had to put up with the noise.

Jock put both arms in the air. "Just getting started. Minnesota touchdown in the first five minutes!"

"It may be a little early to call," said Swan, "but I think Jock Gilman's getting a late Christmas present this year: Vikings and Bears in the NFC championship game."

"You know," Jock said through a mouthful of potato skins, "if you had told me I ever wanted to see Chicago win anything, I'd have said you were crazy. But if it means Minnesota gets to bring the Bears' season to a sad end, then I say bring it on."

"Chicago's just a stepping-stone to the Super Bowl!" Larry said, butting his plastic helmet against Harlan's.

"The Bears are winning, too?" Zack asked. He still couldn't say "Bears" without thinking about Erik the Horrible and the Bears of the North.

"They already won," Swan told him. "Bears beat the Eagles yesterday. And if I was a betting man, I'd say the Vikes are bringing down the Saints today."

"What do you mean if? You *are* a betting man," a female voice called out.

Zack looked over and saw Hillary and Helena North coming in from the kitchen.

Valerie called after them. "Where are you guys going?"

"Just a second," said one of the twins. "I want to see the replay here."

"Yeah, that's what I'm talking about!" yelled Jock when it was over. He reached out and high-fived the twins, one with each hand.

"Hi, Zack," said one twin. "I thought you weren't into watching football."

Zack smiled back, unsure whether it was Hillary or Helena. He liked them both but could never tell them apart. It was the same with Hilda and Helga, the warrior sisters whose tribe was a key ally in the other world.

"Hi," Zack said, looking from one twin to the other.

"It's Helena."

"Right," Zack said, nodding.

Hillary and Helena were friends of Valerie, but Zack got the impression they were here for the game. Hillary accepted a soda from Jock and cracked it open as she sat down on the living-room floor. "So, have you caught a little playoff fever from your dad?" she asked.

"What?" said Zack. His mind had already drifted again, to thoughts of Asleif. "Oh—the game. Uh, yeah." He looked toward the television. "Yeah, it looks like a good one."

Helena grinned. "That's a shaving-cream commercial."

Zack turned away to hide his blushing face. "Right. Well, I'd better . . . "

He started toward his room.

"Hey, where you going?" Jock yelled. "If you stick around

we can do a little four-on-four." He held up a purple-and-gold foam football. Swan, Larry, Harlan, Smitty, Hillary, and Helena were already dividing into teams on either side of the living room.

Zack motioned with his thumb toward his bedroom door. "I just have to, um . . ." Then he turned and slipped away.

When he opened the door to his room, a rush of winter air greeted him. Ollie Grossberg, Zack's best friend, was hanging half over the windowsill.

"What's up?" Zack asked nonchalantly. Ollie used Zack's window as often as he did the front door.

Ollie grunted with one more pull and rolled onto the floor. "I didn't want to try the living room. It sounds pretty crazy out there. I could hear it all the way up the street."

Another muffled roar reverberated through the house.

"Believe me," Zack said. "I know what you mean." He pulled his notes and maps out from the stack of newspapers where he had hidden them and began spreading them out on his workbench. "The one good thing about the playoffs is that it distracts Dad. He's been watching me like a hawk lately."

"I can't really blame him," Ollie said. "You were like a zombie the last time you came back."

Zack remembered it all too well. One minute, Asleif had been taken captive, and the next minute, Zack had found himself back home again, wet and exhausted on his own front lawn. It had been nearly impossible to have a normal conversation with Jock that night. Luckily, Ollie had been there to back him up, and they had slipped off to Zack's room as quickly as possible, saying something about homework. Ever since then, Jock had been extra attentive.

Ollie went on. "You should really tell him about all this. Show him the key. He'll believe you."

Zack looked at Ollie blankly.

"Well, even if he doesn't," said Ollie, "you could try. What's he going to do? Ground you?" Ollie assumed the barrel-chested stance and deep voice of Jock Gilman. "That's it. Your time-travel privileges are gone till you figure out how to appreciate what's important in life. Like football. And, uh . . . things that have something to do with football."

Zack cracked up in spite of himself. He stood up and scratched at an imaginary beard, then rubbed his stomach the way Jock always did. "Yeah, sure, son, I understand. Now, if you'll just put this straitjacket on, we'll go somewhere where they can help you. . . ."

Zack went back to his normal posture. "No way. He would never understand what I'm going through."

"Well, it's not like he could take the key away," Ollie said. "At least if what you told me is true."

Zack fingered the key hidden under his shirt. "Take my word for it. It's true."

More than once, Zack had seen how true. Yggdrasil's Key, it was said, could never be taken by force. The last person to try was a Bear soldier. One pull on the key and it had repelled the man so hard, he had blown through the side of his own ship.

"So meanwhile, what about Asleif?" Ollie asked. He pointed to a sketch Zack had drawn. "She looks just like Ashley Williams, huh?"

"Yeah." Zack looked at the floor. "Just like her."

The difference, which he didn't mention, was that he could speak to Asleif without screwing up. With Ashley Williams, he had gotten as far as anonymously leaving mix CDs for her, but every attempt at conversation had been a disaster.

"Sorry," said Ollie. "I'll stop asking about her."

Ollie was obsessed with the idea of doubles, maybe because his own "double" was Olaf, a three-foot-tall, gray troll. Unlike most of the others, Olaf and Ollie didn't look much alike, but the similarities were undeniable—big ears, short stature, fierce intelligence, and an unlikely self-confidence.

"What about the quest?" he asked. "Two treasures found, one to go, right?"

"Yeah," Zack said. "But Asleif comes first."

"How are you going to convince Jok of that?" Ollie asked.

For Jok the quest was more important than Asleif's life. His primary goal was going to be recapturing Yggdrasil's Chest from Erik the Horrible. The chest already held the first two treasures—the helmet, Faith, and the hammer, Courage. After recovering the chest, Jok's next priority would be to find Sacrifice, which was the third and final treasure.

For Zack, there was only one goal: finding Asleif. He wondered bitterly if Jok would have been as callous about his own wife, Winniferd.

Winniferd of Lykill had disappeared nine years before Zack showed up, but he had heard about her many times. If there was one thing for which Jok seemed willing to surrender the quest, it was Winniferd. He had never stopped looking for her.

And Zack knew that he couldn't stop until he found Asleif. He just wished Jok understood that.

"I don't know what I'm going to do once I get back there," Zack said. "But as long as I'm still here, there's no way for me to find out."

"Well, meanwhile . . ." said Ollie. He pulled a folded piece of paper from the back pocket of his khakis.

"What's that?"

"What's the one thing you wish you could bring with you when you go back?"

Zack thought for a second. "A global positioning system."

Ollie waved his hand in the air as if to erase Zack's idea. "Okay, well, what's the next thing you'd want to have?"

"Night-vision goggles."

Ollie exhaled between his teeth. "Never mind. Look at this." He spread the wrinkled sheet flat on the workbench in front of Zack.

"What is it?"

"Everything else you'd want," Ollie said. He picked up a charcoal pencil and used it as a pointer. "Here's the compass. You said it's always cloudy, so this could be good day or night. And here's a fully loaded Swiss army knife. We won't have to build that part."

"Where are we going to get . . ."

Before Zack could finish, Ollie had pulled the package out of his coat. "I got it at the hobby store this morning."

Zack looked at the box. A picture of the knife showed it splayed open with what looked like two dozen tools. It did in fact look like everything Zack could use, except for night-vision goggles and a global positioning system. "They let you buy this without your parents there?"

Ollie shrugged. "Yeah."

"This is expensive," Zack said. "I can't really—"

"Forget about it," said Ollie. Before Zack could protest, Ollie ripped open the package, spit on the knife's red case, and wiped it off on his jeans. "There. Can't be returned."

Zack smiled at him. It was good having Ollie on his side.

"So anyway," Ollie said, pointing their attention back to his sketch. "If we use minimum-gauge high-tensile wire, it should hold together as one unit, and then each piece can be separately detachable. Here's a shoulder strap, tripod, telescope, and camera."

"Camera?" said Zack.

Ollie shrugged. "I want to see what this Olaf guy looks like."

~⚹~

Zack and Ollie spent the next few hours focused on the multitool. Zack sketched in a few more ideas, and Ollie made a list of places they could look for parts. It felt good to be doing something productive. Zack almost stopped noticing the noise from the living room.

As the afternoon light began to fade, he switched on the tungsten lighting over the workbench. The workbench itself was just an old piece of kitchen counter with two-by-fours for legs, but it suited Zack's purposes. With a little help from his father, he had turned his bedroom into a halfway-decent workshop, including the lights and a large collection of Jock's old tools.

Suddenly the living room seemed to explode with sound. Zack heard the distinct roar of a game-winning moment, and he knew right away—the Minnesota Vikings were one step closer to the Super Bowl.

An instant later, Zack's door flew open. Larry stood with both arms flexed. The ropy tendons in his neck stood out as he screamed.

"Vikings WIN! Oh yeah!"

The door banged against Zack's wall and bounced closed before Larry could take a breath.

Zack scrambled to cover his paperwork. He threw it all back into the stack of newspapers at his side.

"Hang on," he said to Ollie, barking like a sergeant before battle.

Just as Zack knew it would, the door flew open again. It was like a magic trick. A moment earlier, it had just been Larry. Now it was Larry, Swan, Harlan, Smitty, and Jock. They looked like one big, hairy, ten-armed purple-and-gold body, and they sounded like an entire stadium of screaming fans.

"VI-KINGS! VI-KINGS! VI-KINGS!"

Ollie followed Zack's lead as he lunged for the door. They

pushed their way out into the hall, like human bait drawing Jock and his friends away from Zack's room. A moment later, the living room was in chaos.

"VI-KINGS! VI-KINGS! VI-KINGS!"

Zack felt the floor give way slightly as the group jumped up and down. The North twins lifted Jock off the ground with some help from Larry and bounced him like a three-hundred-pound laughing baby. Harlan pulled Valerie into the fray and danced her around the living room. Smitty and Swan toasted each other with soda cans, and a spray of foam shot into the air.

"So, I'm thinking the Vikings won," Ollie shouted into Zack's ear.

Zack shook his head and motioned toward the back door. "Let's get out of here!"

Before they slipped outside, Zack took one more look back. His father stood in the middle of the living room, brandishing a hot dog over his head the way Jok of Lykill swung an ax.

Zack's shoulders tensed against the freezing January air as he shut the door behind him and Ollie. They circled around the house and let themselves back inside through Zack's window.

"It's amazing," Zack said. "How can my father look so much like Jok, and sometimes even act just like Jok, but still be nothing like him? I don't get it."

"Just like everything else," Ollie said.

"Huh?"

"Is there anything about all this that you *do* get?"

A crash followed by the sound of splintering wood and raucous laughter came from the other side of the wall.

"One thing I know," Zack said. "Next football season, I'm living at your house."

CHAPTER TWO

"Are you going to finish that?"

Ollie pointed to Zack's half-eaten lunch, then went back to swabbing the bottom of a pudding cup with his tongue.

Zack looked at the plastic container in front of him. Microwave surprise, his father's specialty. Today, it was a combination of leftover canned beef stew, turkey chili, and what looked to Zack like pigs in a blanket, without the blankets. He pushed it across the cafeteria table and grabbed a handful of Ollie's fries. "You know, Olaf usually gives me half of his food, not the other way around."

"Yeah, and you told me Olaf eats the bugs he picks out of his own ears," Ollie said with his mouth full.

Zack looked around, scanning the cafeteria for the fifth time in as many minutes.

"Gilman, he's not here. Don't you think he'd find you if he was?"

Zack spent most of his time in school these days keeping an eye out for the Free Man.

"I've got a bad feeling about this," Zack said quietly. "I don't think he's coming back this time."

The Free Man had followed Zack between the two worlds

more than once. In the ninth century, the Free Man was a mystic and a hermit, living alone in a cabin of ice that remained frozen in any weather. He was an ally of Jok's tribe, but didn't seem to have any people of his own. In the twenty-first century, he showed up at Zack's school as "Stephan Freeman," an exchange student from Norway. But unlike all the other doubles Zack had met, "Stephan Freeman" was just a guise. The Free Man was the same person wherever Zack saw him. He knew more about the quest than anyone, and had given Zack bits and pieces of information along the way.

The last time Zack had seen him, the Free Man had dropped a few bombshells. He'd said that he'd been searching for Zack for a long time, and that he had left Yggdrasil's Key in the Metrodome parking lot for Zack to find in the first place. What he hadn't said was why.

More disturbingly, he had also suggested that if Zack didn't finish the quest in the past, he might not ever be born in the present. Zack's very existence, it seemed, hinged on finding the third treasure and filling Yggdrasil's Chest. The logic of it all boggled Zack's mind, but the Free Man had been right about everything so far.

Without the Free Man around, Zack felt stranded in the twenty-first century, casting about for clues that didn't surface.

He stood up from the cafeteria table. "I'm going to hit the library again," he told Ollie.

"Yeah," Ollie said sarcastically, "maybe they've got a

whole bunch of new stuff since you checked yesterday."

"Eat your lunch."

Ollie looked up from the mush in front of him. "Technically, this is your lunch," he said with his mouth again full.

"See you later."

The library was deserted, as it always was at lunchtime. Even Mrs. Wasserman, the librarian, was tucked away in her office and didn't see Zack come in. He walked through the stacks, past a dozen or more rows of high bookcases. The Dewey decimal system cataloged Viking books in the 900s, which meant they were in the farthest section against the wall. Zack had his own private spot between the stacks where hardly anyone seemed to go. He reached up, pulled *Viking Times* off the top shelf where he had left it the day before, and settled onto the carpet.

He turned the pages absently, looking for something he hadn't caught before, some mention of the village of Lykill or the Prophecy. Wherever he did find a familiar name, it was always chalked up to mythology—pure fiction, according to these books.

He fingered the key under his shirt and stared at a fanciful diagram of the tree Yggdrasil, its unfathomably huge branches and roots leading from one part of the Norse universe to another.

Fiction, huh?

Zack ran his finger across the page, tracing a path along Yggdrasil's roots where the quest had taken him.

Midgard, land of the humans.

Been there.

Jotunheim, land of the giants.

Been there.

Niflheim, land of the dead.

Zack shuddered, remembering the queen of that world, Hel, and her rotting blue-black legs.

Been there. Not going back.

His finger ended on Asgard, home of the gods, the place where the third treasure was said to be found.

Going there. As soon as I find Asleif.

It all looked so simple, reduced to a single page here in front of him. But finding Asleif was going to be like looking for a miniature needle in nine haystacks. If he could ever get back there at all.

"Hey, Horner, come over here."

Zack recognized the voice right away. Even in a whisper, it made his stomach clench. Eric Spangler, the twenty-first-century version of Erik the Horrible, had slithered into the library. Eric wasn't as dangerous as his ninth-century counterpart, but he was just as obnoxious.

"Whassup?" came another voice.

Doug Horner, Eric's usual sidekick, was there, too. Horner's double, Orn, was a hairy troll with a tendency to lose body parts. Zack had seen Orn lose five toes once, and one arm three different times. Doug Horner still had both arms, but today the left one was in a sling, probably from trying to copy some move he had seen on *Wrestle Fat City.*

Doug Horner and Orn the troll definitely had the lowest combined intelligence of any two doubles Zack had encountered.

Zack hunched down farther against the bookshelf and listened.

"Over here," Eric whispered. They seemed to be a few rows down the stacks.

"Where?"

"Right here. Check it out."

"Don't pull that."

"Why not?"

"I don't feel like going outside."

"Doofus. Who says we have to? What are we going to do—burn up?"

Doug was silent for a moment, then seemed to get the joke. He let out a low chuckle that gave Zack some clue what a laughing gorilla might sound like. A moment later, the fire alarm started to blare.

Zack knew he had two choices—stay put, or leave and cross paths with Eric. Since there was no fire, it hardly seemed worth the hassle.

It wasn't as though he was afraid of Eric. Like most people in school, Eric was almost a foot shorter than Zack's six-foot-three. But he made up for his size by playing dirty and by having the principal, Mr. Ogmund, firmly in his camp. It didn't hurt that Eric's mother was superintendent of schools, and that Ogmund kissed up to the Spangler family as though his job depended on it, which it probably did.

As if on cue, Principal Ogmund's whiny voice came over the public-address system.

"All students should proceed to the nearest exit and convene with your homeroom teacher immediately. Please remain calm."

Ogmund's ninth-century counterpart was a wizard by the name of Ogmunder who was just as much a pawn to Erik the Horrible as Principal Ogmund was to Eric Spangler. Zack hadn't figured out the details, but he was convinced that the wizard was part of Erik's spy network. Maybe he was working with whoever the traitor was in Jok's tribe. Something had to explain how Erik the Horrible was always a step ahead of the game.

The library lights flicked off. Zack heard Mrs. Wasserman pull the door closed behind her as she left. A moment later, a large book flew through the air and smashed into the fire-alarm box, which fell in pieces to the ground. Elsewhere in the school, the alarm continued to wail.

"Excellent!" shouted Doug. "That was even a left-handed throw."

Zack leaned back against the bookshelf and listened in, trying to ignore the anxious churn in his stomach.

"I wish there really was a fire," Eric said. "Then we'd be out for the rest of the day."

Zack heard ripping pages and then Eric's voice again. "I hate this stupid library."

"Yeah," said Doug. "It's so full of . . . um . . . books and stuff."

"So listen," Eric said, changing to a businesslike tone. "My dad got me four tickets. I gave two to Ashley Williams—"

Zack jolted when heard Ashley's name. He tuned his hearing like radar in Eric's direction.

"I left them in her backpack with a note and no name. I just wrote, 'Bring a friend.' Cool, right? One for you, one for me."

"One what? Ticket?"

"Girls, idiot."

Doug laughed lecherously. "Oh yeah, right."

"I just wish the game was in Chicago. My dad could get us into the press box, we'd see the Vikings totally going down, we'd be on the home field when the Bears won—"

"Yeah!" Doug shouted. "Bears rule!" He punched something metal, then shouted out in pain.

Zack leaned back against the books. Ashley Williams? Going to a game with Eric Spangler? She wouldn't actually go, would she? Not that he had any say over what Ashley did. *But still . . .*

The idea of her doing anything with Eric nearly sent Zack's lunch onto the library carpet.

Doug, meanwhile, seemed to be working off some steam. Zack could hear books falling to the ground and Doug's voice getting closer. "Bears are going all the way, man!"

An entire row of heavy volumes rained down on him. Zack crouched forward with his hands over his head. Then, with a sudden impulse, he changed his mind. What was he so afraid of? He stood up and stepped into the open.

23

Eric looked surprised for a second and a half, then gave one of his usual sneers. "What are you doing here, Gutless Gilman? Didn't you hear the fire alarm?"

"Yeah, I heard it," Zack said, returning Eric's stare.

"So what are you waiting for?" Eric said.

"Yeah," said Horner, with his gorilla laugh, "the ice age?"

Now Zack and Eric spoke at the same time. "Shut up, Horner."

Erik took a step toward Zack. His confidence was always a little surprising, the way a Chihuahua will bark at a Great Dane.

"So go on, Gutless," Eric said belligerently. "Go home to your mama." He stopped short and affected a look of confusion. "Oh wait, you can't do that, can you?"

Zack filled up with an instant rage. He reached for Eric. Horner stepped in between them and pushed Zack back several steps.

Zack squeezed his eyes shut for a second. If there was one thing he didn't need right now, it was a fight that would land him in Ogmund's office. Especially not a fight against Eric Spangler. He held up both his hands and took another step away.

"You're not worth the trouble, Spangler."

"Come on," Eric said. He advanced on Zack, backing him up between the bookshelves. "I thought for once in your pathetic life you were going to show a little backbone."

"Go on, Spangler!" shouted Doug. "I got your back. Go for it!"

24

All Zack wanted was to get out of there. Looking at Eric was only a fraction away from looking at the Erik who had stolen Asleif. If he started in on Spangler now, he was afraid he wouldn't be able to stop.

"You're just as gutless as I thought," Eric said. He reached up and grabbed Zack by the front of the shirt.

"Do it, man!" Horner yelled.

"No!" Zack shouted. Along with a handful of Zack's shirt, Eric had also grabbed hold of Yggdrasil's Key. Zack felt its power come alive instantly, like an electrical current through his body.

"What—" It was all Eric could say before the key's force took hold of him. His arms stiffened. His knuckles turned white where they gripped the key with an unbreakable fusion. His eyes bulged and he began to shake all over.

Zack braced himself. Every time this happened, he dreaded it more.

"What's goin' on?" Horner said, in a whine that Zack barely heard.

The key's energy took only a few seconds to run its course. Eric's features froze. His whole body went as rigid as a flagpole. With a sudden explosive force, he flew back against the bookshelf behind him. Zack went in the opposite direction and lost his breath all at once when he slammed against the back wall, then fell to the ground.

He heard more than he saw. Eric hit the tall bookcase and took it down, like the first of several giant dominoes. With a thundering of falling books, the first case fell against the one behind it, and the noise grew. To Zack it sounded something like a stampede as one shelf after another came down. By the time he stood up, Eric was on his back, sprawled across the first of half a dozen empty, fallen cases. The library looked as though an earthquake had hit.

Eric groaned softly, his eyes unfocused. Doug stood a few feet away, making no sound at all as he looked from Eric to Zack and back again. He stepped out of Zack's way when Zack headed for the door.

Out in the hall, students were coming back inside from the false alarm. Zack passed Mrs. Wasserman on her way back to the library. A moment later, her shrill voice sounded up the corridor.

"ERIC SPANGLER! WHAT HAVE YOU DONE?"

CHAPTER THREE

<O_Man: I wish I could have seen it.>
<ZG0091: Like a human bullet, right through the lib.>
<O_Man: Would have been great to get that on tape.>
<ZG0091: Y!!! :)>
<O_Man: Now we know for sure.>
<ZG0091: Know what?>
<O_Man: The key still works.>

Zack pushed back from the computer.

The key still works.

Now that Ollie put it that way, it seemed like the first encouraging piece of news in days.

<O_Man: You still there?>
<ZG0091: Y>
<O_Man: Just wondering. Got to go.>
<ZG0091: Bye.>

Zack clicked onto the Internet and stared at the search screen. He had already tried punching in everything he could think of. Just to keep his fingers busy, he typed "A-S-L-E-I-F."

Heavy footfalls came from upstairs.

"Zack, you down there?"

"Yeah."

The basement steps creaked as Jok came down. Zack erased Asleif's name from the screen in front of him.

"Whatcha doing?"

"I was just talking to Ollie."

Zack did what he could to keep from lying to his father, which meant telling the truth, but selectively.

Jock paused. He giggled and then said, "I got 'em."

Zack knew if he took the bait, he could get stuck in endless conversation. He tried to focus on the computer, but Jock's expectant silence got the best of him.

"Got what?" he asked.

Jock smiled broadly, reached into his back pocket, and held up a fistful of tickets. "Six, count 'em, *six* tickets to Sunday's game."

"How'd you do that?" Zack asked. Even he knew that last-minute playoff tickets were a nearly impossible score.

Jock shrugged. "Just a little purple pride at work. They're not the best seats, but—"

"Last row?"

"No," Jock said defensively, and then, "Third-to-last row. But the point is they are *inside* the stadium." Normally Jock and his crew only made it as far as the Metrodome parking lot.

Something suddenly struck Zack. "Did you say six?"

"That's right." Jock counted the tickets out like money. "Swan, Larry, Harlan, Smitty, me, and . . . the Zack!"

Before Zack could say anything, Jock went on: "Don't even think about it. I already know what you're going to say. This isn't your thing. You don't appreciate the Vikings in quite the same way I do—"

Zack snorted a laugh in spite of himself.

"—but this is a once-in-a-lifetime opportunity."

"Dad, the playoffs happen every year."

Jock held up his hands. "Fair enough. But how often do you get a Vikings–Bears NFC championship played in Minneapolis? Even you have got to be a little interested. Am I right?"

Zack couldn't completely deny it. Something about seeing the Bears lose to the Vikings had a definite appeal, even if it was just football. But still, there was too much to do, and too much to think about.

"Maybe someone else could use the ticket," Zack said. "You could probably sell it for—"

"No way," said Jock. "This one has your name on it."

"I just, um . . ." Zack floundered for an argument. His father took no for an answer about as often as he cleaned house. "I don't think I can go this weekend. I've got homework and . . . stuff I have to do."

"Zaaack." Jock pushed his belly against Zack's chair and started rolling him across the floor.

Zack closed his eyes, searching for patience.

I don't have time for this.

"Seriously, Dad. Thanks, but there's no way—"

"Zaaaaaack."

"Dad!"

He hadn't meant to shout. The tightness in his voice was the kind of tone parents usually used on their kids, not the other way around.

"You don't understand," he said more quietly.

"Oh, I understand," Jock said, still smiling.

"No, Dad. You don't."

Now Jock's voice softened. "Zack, I know you better than you think. I know you've been stressed-out lately, and I know things aren't always easy around here."

Zack kept his mouth shut.

It's not around here that I'm worried about.

Jock put a hand on his shoulder. "I just think maybe if you eased up a little, you know, take life as it comes, have some fun, it might do you some good."

Zack stared at his father, unsure of what to say. He knew Jock was just looking out for him. For all his football mania and bad cooking, it was obvious that Jock Gilman really wanted his kids to be happy. Jock wanted everyone to be happy.

All at once something occurred to Zack. It hit him with a jolt.

His father never would have left Asleif there on that cliff with Erik. Never would have happened.

"Hello? Anyone there?" Jock waved a hand in front of Zack's face.

Zack blinked. It felt like coming back into the room.

"Okay," he said.

"Okay?" Jock asked. "You're coming?"

"Do I have a choice?" Zack asked. "Anyway, it'll be good to see the Bears lose."

Jock laughed and ruffled Zack's thick red hair. "Now *that's* purple pride!" He hummed the Vikings fight song all the way up the stairs and into the kitchen.

When Zack turned back to the computer, a new message was waiting for him. He couldn't tell how long it had been sitting there.

<ANONY-MS.: Did you get the CD?>

He read it three times quickly.

Did I get the CD?

The only CD he had gotten lately was a mix, taped in an envelope to his locker. It had arrived in the same way he had left a disc for Ashley Williams a few weeks before. She hadn't said anything and he hadn't had the nerve to ask her.

"Take it slow, Gilman," he said out loud, then tapped out a reply.

<ZG0091: Yeah, thanks.>
<ANONY-MS.: Good.>
<ZG0091: Who is this?>

Let it be Ashley.

Whoever it was, she knew his screen name and how to find him.

Zack clicked on the name to read the ANONY-MS. profile, but at the same moment, she logged off and was gone. He stared at the blank screen.

If nothing else, he was going to talk to Ashley tomorrow. *Even if I throw up on her shoes, I'm talking to her.*

Zack had always been able to speak to Asleif and still feel like himself. Ashley, on the other hand, left him tongue-tied and frustrated.

Like everything else these days, it seemed more complicated than ever. Asleif was the closest thing to a girlfriend he had ever had, so it wouldn't be right to ask Ashley out, even if the two girls did live over a thousand years apart from each other.

So what am I afraid of?

Maybe speaking to Ashley would only make him feel worse about Asleif.

Or maybe it would give him some kind of clue about finding her again. That seemed like a insane idea, but there wasn't much that seemed sane anymore. He was grasping at straws and he knew it.

After he had found the first treasure, Zack realized, part of him had thought the quest would get easier, or that he would somehow get used to the chaos. But it had only gotten harder and more complicated every step of the way.

He clunked his head down on the computer table, trying to knock away some of the thoughts that crowded his brain—Asleif, the third treasure, the spy in Jok's tribe, Erik the Horrible, Ogmunder . . .

Just take one thing at a time.

That's what Asleif always said.

❧

Zack woke early the next morning. His mind had cleared in the night, but it quickly filled back up as he came awake. He had to get to school, keep looking for the Free Man, try to speak to Ashley Williams, avoid Eric Spangler if he could help it . . .

One thing at a time.

Zack's bedroom window rattled. He looked over, half expecting to see Ollie standing there. Instead, he saw a wall of white, where snow had drifted up against the house. A sharp gust of wind howled outside.

From the kitchen, he heard the drone of a radio announcer.

"Upland High School, closed; Winsdale Elementary, closed; the Whittaker School, closed . . ."

Zack groaned and sat up. Any other time, a snow day would be welcome. Now it was just another obstacle.

He looked at his clock, but the face was blank. When he tried his bedside lamp, it wouldn't turn on. The power outage was no surprise, considering the wind, whistling around the house like a siren.

In the kitchen, Jock stood leaning against the counter with a quart container of ice cream in one hand and a big spoon in the other.

"This stuff's all going to melt," he said.

"What time is it?"

"Six-thirty, maybe. Not that it matters. No one's going

33

anywhere today. You want some eggs? We should finish whatever we can."

"Sure, thanks." Zack pulled another spoon from the drawer and started on the ice cream. It was like chocolate-chip soup. "I need a straw for this."

Jock poured the remainder of the ice cream into two mugs. "There you go. I'll start breakfast."

Zack sat silently while the radio played on.

"This one looks like a record breaker," said the morning-show host.

"Yeah," said a giggly woman.

"We're looking at something like three feet of accumulation before the day's over."

"Wow," said the woman.

"So what are we doing here while everyone else sits at home all nice and warm? It's like a cave in this place."

"Brr," said the woman, again with a giggle.

"It's going to get cold in here, too," Jock said. "We'll have to crank up the fireplace."

The DJ chattered on. "Well, settle in kids, 'cause you're not going anywhere, and neither are we. Coming up after the news, we've got the ten most disgusting things I've ever found in my bathroom. Stick around."

∽✺∾

At nine o'clock, Zack dialed Ollie's number.

"Hey, no school."

"No duh."

"Why don't you come over? We can work on the whatchamacallit." Zack didn't want to say too much out loud with his father right there and his sister somewhere around the house. Jock sat at the kitchen table, eating a half-thawed Salisbury steak on a fork.

"I'll see if my mom will let me go out," Ollie said. "It's crazy out there."

"I'll be in my room," said Zack. "But use the front door. The snow's all the way up to the window."

In the living room, Valerie was trying to start a fire. She had a pile of logs on the andirons and was looking at the cardboard goalpost that still hung limply on the wall.

"Dad, can I burn this thing to get the fire going?"

Jock called back from the kitchen: "No, I want to keep it up till the season's over, for good luck."

Valerie gave it a dubious look. "Good luck?"

"Find something else to use," Jock said.

"Zack, make yourself useful and find me something," she said without looking at him.

"Driftwood burns easily. How about your head?" Zack asked.

"Ha ha," Valerie answered dryly.

Zack headed for the bathroom. "I want to take a shower before Ollie comes over."

"Don't use all the hot water."

"Yeah, yeah."

After a quick shower, Zack smelled smoke from the living room. He looked down and saw a faint waft of it seeping under the bathroom door. He could hear his father and sister shouting.

"What are you talking about? What's a flue?"

"Just go open the door."

When Zack came into the hall, smoke billowed around him.

"Are we on fire?" he called out.

The living room was chilly. Valerie stood waving the front door open and closed while a small drift of snow gathered at her feet. Smoke continued to flow out of the fireplace while Jock reached in with a poker to open up the chimney.

"What did you use for kindling?" Jock grunted.

"Just some newspaper," Valerie said.

"How much newspaper?" Jock asked.

"I don't know," she said. "I just threw a stack in there."

Zack looked around the mostly empty living room. "What newspaper?" he said, afraid of the answer.

"I don't know," Valerie said, "Just whatever you had in your room."

Zack's pulse quickened. "What were you doing in my room?"

He didn't wait for an answer. His bedroom door was standing open when he got there. Among the piles of clothes and books, and the scattered tools and half-finished projects, Zack saw a small blank space on the floor next to his workbench. The stack of newspapers was gone, and with it, all the notes, maps, and drawings he had stashed there so hastily.

I should have put them away. Stupid, stupid, stupid.

He ran back to the living room, where the smoke had begun to clear. Jock stood back wiping his sooty hands on his jeans. In the fireplace, the logs were already burning. Underneath them was a thick layer of black ash.

Zack turned on Valerie. "What did you do?"

Valerie lowered her chin and folded her arms across her chest. "What are you talking about?"

"Why'd you go into my room?"

"Zack, watch your tone," said Jock.

Zack shrugged off his father's hand and stepped toward Valerie. She stared back at him, stony-eyed.

"They were just newspapers," she said. "Calm down."

Just newspapers?

Zack lunged at her. "You don't know anything!"

Jock grabbed him and held him back while Zack continued to yell. "Don't ever, ever go in my room. Ever!"

Not that it was important anymore. Everything was already gone, literally up in flames.

"Sorry," Valerie said, so coldly that it sounded like just the opposite. "What's the matter with you anyway?"

Zack felt his chest heaving against the tight grip of his father's arms. Eventually, his breathing slowed and Jock let go.

"What's going on, Zack?" said his father.

Everything seemed to close in around him. All Zack could see anymore was the front door. "I just need to get out of here."

"Out there?" Jock said, but Zack was already halfway to the door. "Zack!"

Valerie stepped out of his way and he ran outside into the storm.

He pushed blindly across the front lawn as the snow blew around him, enclosing him in its swirl. He barely felt the cold. His father called after him again, but Zack kept going.

Forget it, that's it. I quit.

What was he doing this for? Why did he care? Who was this quest for anyway? A bunch of people who had been dead for over a thousand years, that was who. Even if he could save Asleif, she was already gone, already a skeleton. Dust. History.

Zack's legs kept working as he pushed through snow up to his knees. He couldn't even tell if he was in the street, on the neighbor's lawn, or halfway around the block. The storm encased him. It almost felt good to be so suddenly removed from everything he knew.

He took off the key and stared at it. This was how it had all started, in a snowstorm. All he could see now was white and the key, just like that first day. The day everything fell apart and his life turned upside down.

A wave of anger overtook him, an uncontrollable frustration that was more than just a feeling in his mind. It was like a physical sensation that covered him and blocked out any sense of reason. In that moment, all Zack knew was that everything had gone wrong. Everything he was trying to do was impossible. And he was far worse off with the key than he was without it.

He reached back, and with a power that came from some untapped place deep inside, he threw the key as far into the storm as he could.

It had barely left his fingertips when he realized what a

mistake he had made. His sense of purpose, as clear as ever before, came rushing back to him.

"No!"

He ran headlong into the white blindness of the storm. It swallowed him up just as it had swallowed the key a moment before. But now the key could be anywhere.

The heavy snow resisted Zack's steps as he pushed forward, nearly up to his waist. What had he been thinking? And how was he ever going to find the key again?

The idea of never going back, of not finishing what he had begun, seemed suddenly and infinitely more painful than anything he had been feeling a minute earlier.

Where is it?

He had no idea how far the key might have traveled, or which way it might have gone.

Even if he waited for the storm to be over, he wouldn't know where to come back to. The tight cling of the storm around him gave no point of reference. Not even a tree was in sight.

I found it once. I'll find it again. I have to.

He lurched forward and threw himself into a drift, which covered him completely. He could barely feel the ground with his quickly numbing fingers. When he stood up again, trembling, his sense of direction gone, he was suddenly aware of the cold. Even if he found the key, he could freeze to death out here.

Great. They'll find me with it clutched in my frozen dead hand. Nice ending.

He shut his eyes, searching for some will to keep going. When he opened them, something strange caught his eye. A column of smoke, or steam, several feet ahead in the snow. The wind whipped at it, but he could definitely see something coming up from the ground. He slogged forward, working hard not to lose sight of it.

As he drew nearer, he saw a hole in the snow. It was less than a foot across and sloped inward at the top, as if something had slipped through, and somehow, the storm hadn't covered it back up again. The steam coming up from the hole was barely visible, white on white, but definitely there. It looked like a little chimney in the snow. Like something hot was burning its way down to the ground.

The key. It had sparked to life. Every other time Zack had traveled through time, the key had become amazingly hot. And then Zack realized all at once.

It's going back without me.

CHAPTER FOUR

Zack dove. He landed in the drift, and his bare, nearly numb hand fell onto the key. It felt like a hot stove. He yelled out in pain, but he didn't let go. He couldn't. The key was on the move, and it pulled Zack's two hundred pounds deeper into the snow as if he weighed nothing at all.

A moment later, he was traveling through a bright white crystalline tunnel. More specifically, he was making a tunnel as the key pulled him headfirst through an impossibly huge drift. The ground seemed to have disappeared.

The burning heat of the key in Zack's hand started to seem like nothing compared to the intense ache of the freezing cold all around him. His face, pushing through the snow like a plow, got the worst of it. The sharpest pain was right between his closed eyes, like the mother of all ice cream headaches. He kept his mouth shut, to stop the snow from running down his throat. It felt like frozen gravel as it passed over him, scraping his exposed hands, ears, and cheeks.

He could try to let go of the key, he realized, but where would that leave him? Buried alive? Stuck somewhere in time?

The heavy snow began to break down and turn to slush. As it did, Zack's body surged forward, as if he were sliding down a hill that had just gotten steeper. The slush was even colder than the snow, like an endless ice bath.

Was his body actually moving, or was the world shooting past in the opposite direction? It felt as though miles had gone by. Or maybe the motion he felt was time itself. How long did it take for twelve hundred years to rewind?

Not much longer, I hope.

Zack's lungs constricted, trying to pull in air that wasn't there. His chest tightened like a squeezed sponge. He gripped the key. His thoughts grew fuzzy.

Where is this . . . ? Cold. Stop. Stop.

Somewhere along the way, the slush had turned to water. Zack picked up speed once again. He raced like a torpedo, pulled along by the key. His vague sense of direction told him he had started moving upward. It was too dark in the water to tell. He started to wonder if he was going to reach the ninth century before or after his chest exploded from the lack of oxygen.

All at once the world grew brighter. Zack saw a ceiling of pale blue overhead. He broke through the surface and shot up like a giant piece of toast out of a toaster, twenty feet into the air. His lungs had barely gasped in a breath when he fell back into the water. Sunlight blinded him. He thrashed, trying to get his bearings.

It was warm—or at least, not freezing cold anymore. When Zack finally grew still, he saw that it was a quiet spring or summer day. He was treading water at the base of a cliff, surrounded by an unfamiliar landscape.

Cliffs.

This must have been where he was falling when the key had taken him home the last time. Jok and the others had hit the water, and Zack had fallen back into the twenty-first century.

A hundred feet overhead was the spot where Asleif had been taken.

How long ago?

The springlike weather indicated he hadn't been gone for too long, but was it hours? Days? Weeks later?

Except for his own treading water, everything was quiet. Zack wondered if he was as alone as he seemed to be. Erik the Horrible could be miles away, or he could still be camped at the top of the cliffs, where Zack had last seen him. Jok and his tribe could be close by, or all the way back to Lykill by now.

Yggdrasil's Key, still clutched in Zack's hand, had gone cold again. Zack wasn't surprised to see that it had gone from old and rusted looking to a soft burnished silver, like new. At least he knew he was in the right century.

Start swimming, Gilman.

He put the key around his neck and headed for shore. As he drew near the base of the cliffs, Zack saw a crumpled figure on the rocks. He stopped short in the water. It was too big to be Olaf, but might have been one of his human friends. He clenched back an impulse to shout out.

At second glance, Zack recognized the unmistakable fur cloak of the Bears of the North. The dark matted fur, with a hood made to look like the head of a bear, blocked the man's face. As Zack continued toward shore, he saw two more soldiers, all of them lifeless on the rocks. His hands shook as he stroked through the water, away from where they lay.

The Bear soldiers had probably been climbing down to follow him and the others when they jumped. Or, Zack realized, maybe Erik the Horrible had pushed them over in punishment for letting him get away. That was exactly the kind of thing Erik would do.

Zack slogged out of the water and lay on the shore. The warm sunlight was like a much-needed blanket after his trip. He stayed still for a while, putting off the inevitable.

Someone please just tell me what to do next.

Did he go after Asleif? Go get help from Jok? Would Jok help him get Asleif back, or would he be fixated on Yggdrasil's Chest? Where was Jok? Where was anyone?

Zack had never felt so blind in his decisions before, and they had never seemed as important. After all his wishing and wishing to get back to the ninth century, the answers all seemed as far away as ever.

He stood up and looked toward the top of the cliffs. There was only one place he knew how to reach from here, he realized. The Free Man's cabin. If he could get to the top of the cliff, he could retrace his steps from the last time. It suddenly made sense, especially since the alternative was picking a direction at random. The Free Man would give him some answers. He'd have to.

The cliff was actually a series of outcroppings, like towered steps or shelves. The trick would be climbing from one to the next, but it was better than a sheer wall. Zack put a hand to the rough surface and pulled himself up to the closest ledge. It was just big enough for his toes and the balls of his feet.

He scanned farther up the wall and found his next landing. As he pulled himself up again, sharp rock dug into his palm. A red stain marked the spot where his hand had just been. He wiped the blood onto his jeans and kept going.

For several minutes, the footholds were easy enough to find. Zack got about fifty feet off the ground before he realized he had hit a dead end. Nothing overhead was within reach. His toes pressed into the cliff wall. The ledge where he stood was only a few inches deep.

He checked to either side and saw a way he could go if he climbed down and across before continuing up. His palms stung. A trickle of sweat fell into his eyes, and he swabbed them against his arm.

It was frustrating to reverse direction, but a few minutes later, Zack had worked his way around the dead end. He started up again and reached the widest ledge yet. As he came to it, he saw a large bird's nest built into the side of the wall. Zack was careful not to step on it. Three speckled eggs, the size of chicken's eggs, lay inside. He considered taking them. There was no knowing when or where his next meal was coming from. But the chance of keeping them whole for the rest of the climb seemed remote at best. He also felt a twinge of guilt just thinking about stealing them.

A high-pitched squawk came from overhead. Zack turned his head to see two mottled brown and white birds swoop in his direction. They dive-bombed, narrowly missing his head, then hovered in the air, flapping their wings and screeching.

"All right, all right," he shouted at them. "I wasn't going to take them anyway."

Working to avoid any sudden moves, he climbed on as quickly as he could.

Finally, the top ledge drew near. It looked as though the last maneuver was going to be the hardest. The rocks at the top jutted out from the edge just slightly. Zack was going to have to reach around from below, get a good grip on the edge, and then pull himself up and over the top.

And then hope that Erik isn't waiting for me when I get there.

He climbed past several more nests until he was just beneath the last lip of the cliff. His palms felt as though someone had used sandpaper on them, and his leg muscles were turning to Jell-O. He was going to have to do this quickly.

He braced himself against the wall with his right hand and reached up with his left. Next came the hard part—letting go of the wall. Once he reached up with his right hand, he would have to dangle in the air until he pulled himself up.

Just one quick grab.

He envisioned it in his head, once, then again. His legs quivered. He knew it had to be soon, but still, he couldn't quite get there. He almost wished someone was chasing him. That had always helped before.

Without thinking, he looked down again. His eyes fell on

one of the Bear soldiers on the rocks below. The sight of it was like a force driving him upward. He let his instincts take over. For a stomach-lurching moment, his right arm swung free, then landed solidly on the rock overhead. His feet scraped off the ledge and he felt the full weight of his body hanging in the air.

Adrenaline powered his arms. He pulled himself high enough to see over the edge. The area was clear. No one was around—not that he could turn back now.

He reached forward and pulled himself far enough to lay his chest on flat ground. He took a breath and was just about to swing his legs up over the top, when another gull swooped in. It screeched as it passed and nicked Zack in the forehead. Zack flinched and slid backward. His legs kicked convulsively in the air. His hands ran across the ground as he scrambled to catch hold of something.

An embedded piece of rock lodged under his fingers and he grabbed on, coming to an abrupt halt just short of the cliff's edge. Only a few moments before, he had been hanging in the same spot, wondering if he could pull himself up once. Now he had to do it a second time.

His fingers dug into the ground. He could feel the warmth of blood on his hands, but his grip was solid. The muscles in his arms screamed with pain as he started to pull, but they worked like obedient mules, inch by painful inch.

Finally, he cleared the edge. His clothes, damp with sweat, stuck to him as he rolled onto flat ground. He pounded the earth with his fist, feeling strangely triumphant and frustrated. Did everything have to be such a struggle?

He scanned the nearby woods. Last time, the Bears had ambushed them from out of nowhere. He'd have to be on his guard.

Behind him, the landscape stretched away from the cliffs. A range of knobby pale green hills rolled toward the horizon, where a thin line of sea shimmered in the afternoon sun. It was a beautiful sight, but all Zack could see was the vastness of it. Asleif was out there somewhere.

He put a hand to his chest and felt Yggdrasil's Key, still there. That was always reassuring. Without that key, he'd be lost in this world even if he did find Asleif—it was only with the key that he was able to understand the language everyone here spoke. Zack reached his other hand out and propped himself up, wishing for a cheeseburger and a day off.

But this day, it seemed, was just beginning.

CHAPTER FIVE

Find the river, get upstream, find the Free Man, find Asleif.

Zack repeated the plan to himself like marching orders. He backtracked through the woods, where he and Asleif had run from the Bears' ambush the last time. Memories of that day clung like the brambles pulling at his pant legs in the underbrush.

Soon enough, the enormous ridged edifice that was one of Yggdrasil's great roots showed through the trees. Zack picked up his pace, and came out at the edge of a wide, slowly flowing river. The giant tree root ran across the far side like a canyon wall. Beneath it, Zack knew, was a tunnel. They had followed it the last time, down to the land of the dead and back again. A familiar, foul-smelling mist poured out of the ground at the tunnel's entrance.

Well, at least I'm not going that way.

Zack turned gratefully away from the smell and headed upriver.

The sun was still high. If he was lucky, he could get at least halfway to the Free Man's ice cabin by nightfall.

For several hours, the giant tree root ran along the far side of the river. Eventually, it curved away, replaced by gently sloping hills. Dense forest continued on Zack's side of the water.

As daylight turned golden and shadows lengthened, the temperature began to drop. Zack's jeans and flannel shirt were dry but thin. He had left the house so angrily that morning, he hadn't bothered to put on a coat. The best thing he could do to stay warm was to keep moving for as long as he could.

Jok and the others always used striking stones to start fires. Now Zack wished he had paid more attention when they'd done this. He was probably surrounded by all the right supplies and didn't even know it.

The day disappeared quickly. A few stars and a pale half-moon emerged in the darkening sky. Zack's pace slowed. More than once, something caught his foot and he went down.

The only thing that seemed worse than continuing in the dark was the idea of sleeping on the cold ground. A thick blanket of misery settled over him.

Somewhere in the middle of the night, Zack tripped again and didn't get up. He didn't have the energy to yell, or cry, or even get angry. He lay on the ground, his mind dulled, his body glad just to stop moving. A moment later, he was asleep.

❧

He woke up in a ball. It was morning but still dim. When he rolled over, every muscle complained.

This must be what it's like to be old—like three hundred years old.

He heard himself groan the way his father did sometimes. His neck didn't want to turn, his elbow felt permanently welded into a bent position, and his leg was still asleep where it had been draped over a rock. The only thing roaring to life was his stomach, which greeted the day with an energetic growl.

He hobbled over to the river and drank deeply.

Water. Nice breakfast.

Twenty-four hours with no food. Even the water seemed to betray him. He could hear it sloshing in his empty stomach. A stitch in his side stayed with him as he continued upriver.

Halfway through the morning, he came to the rapids he and the others had ridden, going the other way. White water churned and exploded against a maze of boulders studding the riverbed. It was hard to imagine how they had come through it alive. Zack stuck to the forest, away from the water's edge. Once through those rapids had been more than enough.

When the sound of rushing water died away, he made his way closer to the river. At last, he was making some noticeable progress.

After another hour or more of wading in shallow water on slick rocks, Zack noticed two roughly hewn tree stumps at the top of the sloped bank on his right. Harald and Sigurd had chopped them down, and they had all used the logs as makeshift rafts to float downstream.

Zack found it somehow reassuring, but also hard to imagine,

that they had all stood on this spot together, however long ago it had been. In a way, it seemed like forever. That was before he suspected any of them of being a spy, before he realized how expendable human life was to Jok, and long before they had lost Asleif.

"Asleif."

He said her name out loud. It was all he needed to push himself on.

Get upstream. Find the Free Man. Find Asleif.

Finally, he found what he was looking for. Up on the high bank, among tall reeds, the underbrush had been cut away. He remembered Jok using his sword to bushwhack as they neared the river. This was where the Free Man had left them.

Backtracking through the brush was surprisingly easy. Zack's tribe mates weren't exactly light on their feet. They had left a clear trail. That it was clear told Zack that little time had passed since his last visit. Nothing had grown back.

He followed through tall grasses, and more thorny undergrowth, then into a familiar pine forest. The ground eventually sloped upward and Zack found himself on an actual trail, blazed into a mountainside. The Free Man's mountain. He ran a few steps, then walked, then ran some more. Anything to get there sooner.

The forest opened up and he jogged into the clearing where he knew the Free Man's cabin to be—but the cabin was gone. The ground was a swampy mess of mud and turf.

The cabin hadn't disappeared. It had melted.

Zack dropped to his knees. Even if the Free Man hadn't been home, Zack had been counting on finding some food and a place to rest. This new twist was a sucker punch in the gut—just one more thing he hadn't seen coming.

Zack pounded the wet ground. He yelled out in frustration. The empty clearing looked onto a deep valley, and he heard his own voice echoing back at him, as if to say, *You're the only one here, you're the only one here. . . .*

He couldn't even give up if he wanted to. There was no surrender here, no "game over." One way or another, he had to deal with this. He put a hand to Yggdrasil's Key, and wondered when it would be taking him home again.

But he couldn't go home either. He still had business here. He was going to have get back to Lykill, somehow. He had made the trip twice before—once, following Olaf, and another time, following Jok through the darkness. This time, he would have to do it on his own. It was best to just keep moving.

As he turned to go, something caught his eye. Two shapes in the distance, coming across the valley toward him. The muscles in his legs seized as dual impulses told him to duck for cover, and then to stay where he was.

Then he tensed again, with excitement. The shapes in the distance took form. They were two enormous black ravens, flying across the valley faster than any ordinary birds could ever fly. It was Huginn and Muninn.

"Hey!"

Zack shouted and waved like a castaway flagging down a plane. "Hey! Over here!" The closer the ravens drew, the more excited he became. Anything familiar would have been a relief. Finding Huginn and Muninn, however, was like hitting the jackpot.

The two ravens had been a huge help to Zack on more than one occasion. His research at home had told him that they were the eyes and ears of Odin, king of all the gods. They knew more about what went on in this world than anyone.

A stiff wind blew over Zack as they landed on the ground nearby. Each raven was as tall as Zack himself, with a wingspan of at least twenty feet across. Their shining black eyes were like enormous marbles.

"There's no need to scream," said one of the birds. "Did you think we couldn't see you?"

"We were coming to meet you," said the other.

Zack nodded vigorously. "Right," he said, smiling widely. "Sorry. I just can't believe you're here." In his head, Zack was speaking English, but he could hear the Old Norse coming out of his mouth, and feel the strange shapes of the words. As long as he held Yggdrasil's Key, Zack knew, he could both speak the language and understand what others were saying, including the two ravens.

"Well, we almost weren't here," said one of them. "Huginn thought it best to fly east this morning. We've just come through the worst thunderstorm in all the nine worlds."

"Not at all," snapped Huginn. "Muninn *thinks* that was what I said, but Muninn would do well to listen more attentively."

"Listen? It's all I do," said Muninn. "If you stopped speaking for even a moment, I might get a bit of peace."

"Don't tell me about peace," started Huginn, and the two began squawking at each other. Zack could hear only snatches now as their high-pitched voices grew even more shrill.

"I don't—"

"If I ever—"

"The worst thing—"

"Keep your beak shut—"

Zack looked back and forth, as if he were watching a tennis match. Finally, he grew impatient and broke in.

"Hey!"

The birds stopped and looked at him calmly, as if they hadn't been arguing.

"I just . . . I'm . . ." He wasn't even sure what to ask, and his stomach took over for him. "Do you know if I can eat anything around here?"

"Yes, yes, of course," said Huginn, his manner suddenly businesslike. He hopped across the clearing to a large, fallen tree branch lying in the mud. With one great peck of his giant beak, he split the log in two. Zack walked over and looked at it skeptically. Several dozen yellowish-brown wormlike bugs writhed within the moist tree flesh. His empty stomach twisted inside.

"You're kidding, right?"

"Grubs are very nutritious, for humans and animals alike," Huginn said.

Zack wanted to say no thanks, but the ache in his belly was stronger than anything else right now. He reached down and picked up one of the grubs. It wriggled in his fingers.

Oh man. Just a big jelly bean, that's all.

He held his nose and gobbled the thing down, nearly whole. The earthy taste was something like dirt, but it felt good just to swallow something. He tried not to think about what he was doing, and forced down several more. He stepped back from the log and shook his head.

"You guys eat these all the time?" he asked, choking down the last bits of grub left in his teeth.

"Us?" Muninn said. "No, of course not. Grubs are disgusting. We are well fed at home in Asgard."

"Now to business," said Huginn. "It is time for you to bring the Prophecy to a close."

And then, as if by some invisible cue, the birds began reciting the Prophecy in singsong unison.

"Yggdrasil's Chest, Yggdrasil's Key,
And Lost Boy will unite as three,
Beginning then the glory quest
That opens with Yggdrasil's Chest.

"Glory found is glory earned
And what is Lost must be returned.
Size of a man, this Boy will be,
And with him comes Yggdrasil's Key.

"With the key there comes a price:
Courage, Faith, and Sacrifice.
The way is far, the road will bend
The Boy will lead until the end."

Zack waited patiently. It was best not to offend the ravens when he needed them most, and they always seemed to love reciting the Prophecy.

Finally, he said, "What about Asleif? Do you know where she is?"

"She is with Erik the Horrible," Huginn said plainly.

Zack's heart leapt. Finally, some definite news. "Is she all right?" he nearly shouted.

"She is alive," said Muninn. "We can only tell you what we see from the air."

"We are not interpreters," added Huginn.

"Don't put it like that," said Muninn. "We're not idiots."

"Well you're half right," said Huginn. "*I'm* not an idiot."

Again, the two birds set to screeching at each other.

"What about Jok?" Zack yelled. "Where's my tribe?" It was probably best to get as much information as possible as quickly as possible. The ravens didn't always stick around for long.

Huginn turned to Zack while Muninn was still screeching. "Jok is in Lykill with the others."

"What about the Free Man? Where is he?"

"The Free Man—" started Huginn, who was then interrupted by Muninn.

"The Free Man is on his own business. He isn't—"

Now Huginn interrupted. "You speak too much." He turned to Zack. "We don't know where the Free Man is."

"*I* speak too much?" said Muninn. He puffed the feathers on his chest and turned away.

"And how far is Asleif from here?" Zack pressed.

Huginn started to answer, but Muninn jumped in. "Not far. Erik's camp is to the west. He seems to be moving toward the third root of Yggdrasil."

"Is he going after the third treasure already? He doesn't have this."

Zack held up Yggdrasil's Key.

"We can't tell you what his thoughts are," Muninn snapped.

Zack put his hands to his head and tried to strategize quickly. If he could get to Lykill and convince Jok to make a priority of rescuing Asleif, then he'd have Jok's whole tribe for backup. But there was no guarantee Jok would agree. Zack still couldn't shake the image from his mind of Jok knocking him off the cliff to stop him from saving Asleif while he still had a chance to do so. Meanwhile, a lot could happen while Zack was traveling to Lykill. Asleif might be lost forever.

It was a gamble either way, but Zack had come to only one conclusion. He was going after Asleif on his own.

CHAPTER SIX

"Wait!" Zack called after Huginn and Muninn. They stood on the edge of the clearing, ready to take off. "I need your help."

Muninn cocked his head and looked sideways at Zack. "Our help? Haven't we already—"

"Just one more favor. Please. I don't have any time."

Now that Zack knew where Asleif was for sure, any delay seemed like too much.

"Why don't I like the sound of this?" muttered Huginn.

"Because you only like the sound of your own voice," answered Muninn.

"What is the favor?" Huginn asked.

Zack took a breath. "I need a ride."

"You do it," both birds said to each other at once.

"I carried him the last time," Huginn put in right away.

"For all of a moment," Muninn sniped.

Zack jumped in again, choosing his words carefully. The ravens were unpredictable, but one thing about them was always the same.

"What about a little competition?" he asked. "Maybe see who could carry me the farthest?"

Huginn made a clucking sound in his throat. "Lost Boy,

don't you think we can see what you're doing? Trying to take advantage of us? We are not supposed to—"

"I'll compete," Muninn said.

Huginn snapped his beak shut and looked at Muninn. "Typical," he said. "Just like you. Muninn, our role here is clear. We are not supposed to—"

"So I am the winner," said Muninn.

At that, Huginn turned abruptly to Zack. "I will compete first."

❧

Zack sat at the edge of the clearing, holding fast to Huginn's legs. With a birdlike grunt and a heave, Huginn flared his wings. They left the mountainside with a lurch. The raven tucked his legs like landing gear, pulling Zack's arms uncomfortably but securely into place.

A moment later, they were soaring across the valley. The wind had a cold bite to it, but Zack was just glad to be riding instead of hiking. He glanced down at his feet, with the ground far below. It almost looked as though he was stepping across a miniature landscape.

"This way," Muninn called out insistently.

Huginn grunted in reply, then banked in Muninn's direction. Zack felt his stomach tilt and contract. He pressed his mouth closed. The only thing worse than eating grubs would be throwing them back up again. Huginn glided and flapped, glided and flapped, each surge sending another wave through Zack's belly.

Despite the fluttering stomach, Zack felt lighter than his two hundred pounds. The odds of finding Asleif and bringing her back to Lykill had just improved dramatically. A sense of possibility crept into his mind for the first time in days.

"How far to Erik's camp?" he called out.

"Beyond the horizon," Muninn called back.

The land was a patchwork of forest and hills, woven with lakes and rivers in every direction. From this height, Zack couldn't even guess how many miles he was looking at.

A few minutes later, Huginn began to lose altitude. The surge of his wings was less energetic with each flap.

"Are you ready to stop?" Zack called up. "Do you want to land?"

"Why land?" said Muninn, dipping down next to them. "I thought you were in a hurry."

"I am," Zack said, "but—hey!" Huginn's legs began to unfold, loosening Zack's grip.

"What are you doing?"

"Muninn's . . . turn," Huginn said weakly.

"Wait!" Zack yelled in a panic. "It doesn't have to be in mid—"

Huginn flicked his legs with one quick motion and Zack fell free.

"AIIIIIIIIIIR . . ."

His yell became a soundless gasp as the air sucked out of his lungs. The ground rushed toward him and he swung his arms around as if he might find something to grab on to.

"Be still!" screamed one of the birds. Then, with a clean snatch, Muninn plucked him out of the air. Zack swooped back up like a sky diver opening his chute. It took several seconds for his mind to catch up and his panic to stop firing.

"Don't do that!" he yelled, as if it mattered now.

It was hard to hear above the wind, but it sounded as though both ravens were snickering. "You fall like a stone, Lost Boy," said Huginn.

"Yeah, well, now you know," Zack grumbled, squirming for a more comfortable position.

The second flight didn't last as long as the first. Soon Muninn was gliding longer and flapping less frequently than before.

"Ha!" Huginn yelled out. "I am the winner!"

"Fine," grunted Muninn. "Take him back, then."

Before Zack could object, he suddenly noticed several thin columns of smoke in the distance, and what looked like rows of tents.

"Erik's camp. Over there!"

He pointed instinctively, and his arm slid down Muninn's leg. Muninn screeched. They listed sharply to the side.

"What are you doing?"

"Sorry!"

Zack tried to pull himself back up, but he only threw them further off balance. With a sudden change of direction, they swung around and collided with Huginn, who had swooped in closer.

A cocoon of black feathers closed around Zack. He

reached blindly for anything to hold on to while they tumbled and spun downward as a group. All he could hear was high-pitched screeching.

"Let go!"

"I can't!"

"What are you doing?"

"Get off me!"

The two birds came apart and Zack saw the tops of the trees, much closer than before. He also found that he had taken hold of both ravens, locking them all together. It was him they were yelling at.

"Lost Boy, let go!"

In the confusion it was impossible to know what to let go of and what to hang on to. His feet brushed hard against the pointed top of a pine tree as they flew over it. Another, taller tree was dead ahead.

"Up! Up!" Zack shouted.

The ravens pulled away from each other. With a rush of horror, Zack felt both of his hands come free. His forward momentum carried him straight into the tree, which caught him like a giant, spiny hand. Branches splintered and cracked. Pine needles scrubbed his face and arms. His body came to a sudden stop, entwined with the tree and suspended nearly upside down.

"You weakling."

"Idiot!"

"Coward!"

"Sparrow!"

"I'm going home."

"Fine."

Zack heard the ravens' voices, fading to the distance. The last thing he heard was, "Good luck, Lost Boy!"

He scrabbled with his arms to get hold of something—anything. He pulled on the nearest branch to upright himself. Almost immediately, it bent to the side. Zack slid farther down inside the tree, breaking off small branches as he went. He came to a rest against a larger limb, but only for a second. With a sickening crack, the branch gave way and he was falling again. Suddenly he came to another stop, wedged between two limbs that grew out from the trunk in a V shape.

Too dazed for panic, Zack rolled his head, trying to figure up from down.

The ground was twenty or thirty feet below. From this height, he realized, he could still see the smoke from Erik's camp. That smoke meant Asleif was somewhere nearby. The thought of it cleared his mind.

It was a quick climb down, and Zack nearly kissed the earth when he got there.

No more flying.

Everything had been moving so fast, the forest felt unnaturally still. Other than the wind whisking softly through the trees, there was no sound. Zack realized he could actually smell the campfires now. He knew that Jok and his tribe could navigate their ship by smell in the dark. Maybe he was developing Viking instincts.

He held up a handful of pine needles and sprinkled them

over the ground to see which way the wind was blowing. The needles floated back toward him and landed at his feet. If nothing changed, the wind would bring the smell of smoke his way as he moved toward the camp.

He set off again, treading cautiously, pausing every hundred feet or so to check his progress. The smell of smoke grew stronger. He saw roughly hewn tree trunks where wood had been chopped hastily. All at once the sound of voices stopped him cold. The words weren't clear, but it meant he was close enough to be caught.

Darkness was coming on quickly, and this time Zack was glad for it. Erik's camp lay beyond the edge of the forest on an exposed patch of land. He stayed low just behind the last line of trees.

Two dozen or more tents were set up at the mouth of a pass, which cut between overlapping gravel-covered hills. Beyond them, Zack could see higher, rocky formations silhouetted like towers against the orange twilight of the sky.

Dark, fur-cloaked figures passed through the camp. Many more were gathered around several fires, which showed like bursts of light between the rows of tents. Next to the largest fire, near the center of camp, a banner hung on a high pole, red on one side and black on the other. Erik the Horrible's colors. But no sign of Erik himself, or of Asleif.

Zack scanned the camp, trying not to think about how outnumbered he was. Another smell reached him—roasting meat. He put a hand to his stomach.

No growling.

If there was any chance of grabbing some food, he would do it.

Then something else came through the evening air—the sound of Asleif's harp. Zack had heard her play several times before, back in Lykill. The softly flowing melody was unmistakable. His heart thudded heavily in his chest where he lay on the ground. And then, as if Asleif were reaching out to him, she began to sing.

> *"None so wise, nor brave nor strong*
> *As he, the one we honor here.*
> *With fiery fists and iron hand*
> *Erik we shall all revere."*

Zack clenched his jaw against the anger that rose up in him. Despite the words Asleif sang, he swore he could hear the bitterness in her song. Erik had made her his slave once again.

But not for long.

CHAPTER SEVEN

Zack left the forest and moved in toward Erik's camp. Out in the open, he depended more on the growing darkness than on anything else for cover. He crept halfway to the outermost row of tents and then lay down, trying to home in on Asleif's voice.

Keep singing. Keep singing.

Between the tents, he saw more campfires and dozens of Bear soldiers gathered around them. Most had heavy swords at their sides and drinking horns in their hands. One soldier with a long braid down his back sat sharpening an ax blade. The metal made a hissing, snicking sound against the whetstone in his hand.

"When this is through, I'll get myself a proper halberd," said the soldier.

"When this is through, you'll probably be dead," growled another.

Several others laughed, so casually it put a chill up Zack's spine. Staying low, he continued around the camp, keeping his distance. Asleif stopped singing but continued to strum her harp. Zack followed the sound.

He came around another row of tents, and suddenly there she was.

Asleif!

It was all he could do not to shout out to her.

She sat alone and unbound in front of a fire, absently fingering the harp strings, with her eyes on the sky. Her dark hair hung back from her head against her shoulders. She looked almost peaceful as she strummed, the firelight playing warmly over her soft expression. Her face wasn't bruised or cut. That was good.

She wasn't chained or tied either, which meant there was probably a guard nearby.

Zack shuffled across the ground on his stomach, several feet closer, but still too far to whisper to Asleif. The nearest tent was about twenty feet away, and Asleif was another twenty or so beyond that.

All right, Gilman, this is it.

His mind raced. What if she were taken away right now? What if he couldn't reach her in time, after all this? The idea of it spurred him on. When another burst of laughter came from across camp, he dashed to the back of the closest tent, using the noise as cover. His ragged breath and pounding heart were a strange contrast to Asleif's calm music.

He peeked around the corner and got a clear view of her face. It made him want to jump up, grab her, and run. But this had to be just right. If he surprised her too much, she might yell out.

He rose up onto one knee, ready to make his move, but then paused at the sound of footsteps. Several Bear soldiers were approaching Asleif.

68

"Keep playing, girl. You wouldn't want to upset the little man."

The others laughed coarsely.

"You keep your tongue before someone takes it from you in the night," snapped Asleif.

Zack's heart surged with a rush of pride. She sounded as though no one could get the best of her. There was no defeat in her voice.

The soldiers laughed again, but moved on. Asleif resumed her playing.

Zack leaned out again where he could see her. As softly as he could, he whispered her name.

"Asleif."

Her fingers paused on the strings for a moment then kept going.

"Asleif," he tried again, a tiny bit louder.

Asleif turned her head slowly as she continued to play. Her eyes met Zack's, and opened wide in silent surprise. Without any interruption to the music, she turned and looked farther into camp where Zack couldn't see. When she looked back, she nodded. The coast was clear.

Zack waved for her to come his way, but she motioned with her head toward her own feet. Zack looked down, but the shadows and her long skirt made it hard to see. She was probably bound at the ankles, he realized. This would have been a good time to have the all-purpose tool he and Ollie had been working on. If only he'd had it with him when the key heated up.

Flashlight, screwdriver, chisel . . .

He would have to go on without any of them.

As Zack moved tentatively forward, Asleif kept her gaze on the camp, playing and nodding, indicating it was safe to continue. The hard lump of anxiety in his chest rose as he grew nearer. His breath was shallow. He forced himself to concentrate.

Stay steady.

Asleif didn't even look at Zack as he crawled the last few feet on his belly. He reached out and felt around her ankles for the chain, but nothing was there. An alarm went off in his head.

Something's wrong.

Asleif screamed.

Zack looked up and he saw three Bear soldiers coming through the camp toward them. He jumped up, panic threatening to overtake him, and pulled Asleif to her feet.

"Come on!" he urged her. The soldiers were nearly upon them. He turned and almost ran into three more Bears coming from the other direction, then jumped back as they closed in from either side. Their swords were already out. One of the soldiers grinned, showing a checkerboard of black spaces and yellow teeth.

"Looks like we caught something, boys," he said.

Zack clawed at the cord around his neck and pulled out the key. It was the closest thing he had to a weapon. "Stay away!" he yelled, holding it in front of him. If anyone tried to take it, he could blow them back and maybe open up a hole in the circle. The Bears sneered and growled, but didn't come any closer.

Asleif stood perfectly still, as if she were in shock. Zack pressed his shoulder against hers while he kept his eyes on the Bears, trying not to show his own confusion. He had no idea what to do next.

Then something hard caught him on the back of the head. He heard a crunch and felt a sharp pain run down his neck. A moment later, someone tackled him from behind. His knees buckled and he was suddenly under the huge weight of several soldiers.

He yelled, "Asleif!" But the sound was muffled. Strong hands grabbed his arms and legs, rolled him over, and pinned him.

A shooting pain throbbed in Zack's head. He couldn't see Asleif anymore. The soldiers crowded around, blocking his view. They held him down but didn't try to take the key. The Bear nearest to it knelt on Zack's forearm.

Zack lay still. Struggling against so many was just a waste of strength.

How had this gone so wrong? Less than a minute before, they had been nearly home free. Now Asleif was gone again, out of sight. All Zack could see were unshaven, leering faces. This close, he also noticed that several of the soldiers had oddly shaped burn marks on their cheeks. The one holding down his right arm had the same kind of scar on both sides of his face. Some kind of punishment maybe.

"So the Lost Boy is found again."

There it was. Erik's voice. It pushed into Zack's racing mind like a splinter.

Erik stepped through the crowd. He motioned for the soldiers to pull Zack up to his knees, which they did, while four others kept him at sword point.

"Where's Asleif?" Zack demanded.

Erik ignored the question. His expression, as always, looked as though he had a bad taste in his mouth. He carried his usual staff—a shoulder-height iron rod, pointed at the bottom, with a carved torch at the top made to look a skull. Flame showed through its open mouth and empty eye sockets.

A cloak the color of dried blood hung from his narrow shoulders, trimmed with black fur and a line of small white bones that clattered on the ground as he began pacing in front of Zack.

"I have to say, even I'm surprised at your stupidity," he taunted. "Coming in like this without an invitation seems like an especially bad idea." He drove the pointed end of his staff into the ground, then leaned down to look at Yggdrasil's Key, still clutched in Zack's hand. Zack pulled it away but then felt a sharp warning jab in his side.

"It's all right," Erik said. "I'm not going to try to take it. We all know where that leads, don't we?" Several soldiers laughed uneasily.

"Go ahead." Erik motioned for Zack to put the key back on.

Zack eyed him suspiciously, but it was better to put it on than risk dropping it. Without the key, he wouldn't be able to understand a word anyone was saying. As soon as he had it around his neck, someone grabbed his hands from behind and roughly tied them together. Coarse rope dug into his wrists.

Erik took his staff out of the ground and waved the torch end back and forth in front of the key. Zack could feel the heat of the flame through his shirt. It gave him some idea where the burn scars on the Bears' faces had come from.

"'Yggdrasil's Chest, Yggdrasil's Key, and Lost Boy will unite as three,'" Erik said slowly, quoting from the Prophecy.

"How do I know you still even have the chest?" Zack said, not really expecting an answer.

"It's not important that you know," Erik said. "What's important is that I *do* have all three—the chest, the key, and you—and now we can finish this once and for all."

Zack tried to stay calm. All he could think about was wiping the smug expression off of Erik's face. "Okay," he said. "You've got what you want. Now let Asleif go."

Erik's sneer turned to something that resembled a smile. "Asleif!" he called.

"I'm right here." Her voice came from somewhere in the crowd of Bear soldiers. She had been there all along. When she pushed through to stand next to Erik, her hands weren't tied. She stood straight, with her gaze on the ground.

Zack stared at both of them, and an ugly realization began to take form.

"Asleif," Erik said. "You're free to go."

Asleif didn't move.

Zack shut his eyes, fighting back what he didn't want to believe.

No. No way. No no no.

"She's very good," Erik said. "Very convincing. Actually the whole story was her idea. Wasn't it, Asleif?"

Zack stared at Erik, unable to take it all in. How was this possible? He slumped forward, as if everything holding him up had just been pulled away.

No no no no no.

Erik went on coolly. "An escaped slave girl, taken in by Jok of Lykill. Poor Jok. He was so pathetic, so anxious to be a hero, he never even gave it a second thought."

Finally, Zack looked up at Asleif, but she still wouldn't look back at him.

"How could you do this?" he asked. Somehow, she looked the same and completely different all at once. He knew he should hate her, but it was too far a leap to make all at once. He just wanted what he was seeing not to be true.

"It was you? Spying for Erik all this time?" he asked weakly.

Finally, she looked at him. Her jaw set in a familiar stubborn expression, though Zack saw it differently than he ever had before. If she was sorry, her face didn't show it.

"I had some help on this end," she said. Her voice was like acid in Zack's stomach. "Lost Boy, it wasn't—"

"Be quiet," Erik snapped, cutting her off. "Come."

Soldiers pulled Zack to his feet, but he didn't stand. They dragged him by the armpits across camp. Zack looked dully at the ground. What he had just learned consumed him.

How could they have never known? How did she do this?

The first parts of the quest passed through his mind, and he turned them over, trying to see them in his memory for what they really were. No wonder Asleif had always insisted on coming with Jok and his men. Zack's chest tightened, thinking how he had let himself believe it was because she liked him.

He barely noticed where the Bear soldiers were taking him. Soon they came to a large tent in the center of camp. Zack heard a soft whimpering from inside.

They passed through the flap door and he recognized Ogmunder the Wizard, even from behind. His tall thin frame, the same as Mr. Ogmund from school, was hunched over a large worktable in the center of the tent. Lying on the table was Orn, Erik's main henchman and the source of the whimpering. A wet, green gash showed on the side of his head where his ear would normally be. The rest of him was covered in dark fur. Orn always looked to Zack like a cross between a gorilla and Doug Horner from home.

"Keep still," Ogmunder said testily, holding the ogre down. "Unless you want this new ear to grow out of your forehead."

"Ogmunder!" Erik barked.

"Not now," Ogmunder said, his back still to them. He poured a small vial of clear liquid onto the side of Orn's head. Zack heard a low sizzle and saw smoke coming from the wound. Orn pounded the table with both fists and yelped in pain.

"Maybe you'll learn to listen this time and I won't have to cut it off again," Erik said.

Ogmunder wiped his hands on his robe and turned around. His eyebrows went up when he saw Zack. "Well, this is interesting,"

"I need for him to sleep well tonight," Erik said.

Ogmunder looked Zack over, sizing him up. "I'll need something strong for a boy this hefty." He went to a table at the far side of the tent, loaded with bowls, jars, small boxes, and what looked like a pile of dead fish. Several small cages were also stacked in the corner, holding dozens of mice, other rodents, and birds.

"What is this? Your laboratory?" Zack said.

"That's none of your concern," snapped Ogmunder.

One of the Bear soldiers behind Zack spoke in a hushed voice. "What's a laboratory?"

"Quiet!" Erik said. In one quick motion, he reached over with his torch and lit the soldier's cloak. The sharp smell of scorched Bear fur filled the tent.

The soldier yelled out and shrugged off the burning cloak, then stamped it out on the ground. No one else moved.

"Can we *please* do one thing at a time here?" Erik said.

Asleif, meanwhile, stood next to a large cage in the tent. Inside were half a dozen gray-and-white birds. She twittered at them and they began chirping immediately.

Zack realized he had seen the same kind of birds before. Asleif had spent hours with them at home in Lykill. She had told him once that they inspired her music. Zack watched her, wondering bitterly if even that was a lie.

"You should make her keep those infernal birds in her own tent," Ogmunder said over his shoulder. He had begun mixing ingredients from several small pots. "They're a nuisance in here."

"Stick to your business if you want to get paid," Erik said.

"I'm still waiting for that," muttered Ogmunder.

"Wait a second," Zack said suddenly. "Those birds . . ."

"Cover them up," Ogmunder barked. He pushed Asleif aside and tossed a thin cloth over the cage. The birds grew quiet.

"Fool," said Asleif. She backhanded one of Ogmunder's tall clay pots and knocked it to the dirt floor, where it broke into several pieces. Then she turned and walked out of the tent.

"She'd best mind her manners," Ogmunder said. "I have half a mind to drown those birds."

"Fine with me," Erik said. "They've served their purpose."

Zack was almost glad Asleif was gone. It hurt just to look at her. He stared at the covered birdcage as a theory came together in his mind. Were they some kind of homing pigeon?

"Is that how you spied?" he asked Erik, pointing to the cage. "With those?" He couldn't help blurting out his questions. Now he really wanted to know.

Erik seemed unable to help himself either. He smiled proudly. "It wasn't hard," he said. "None of your idiot friends in Lykill could read her messages, even if they had found one."

Zack tried not to show any emotion. It was true, though. No one in Lykill could read or write, besides himself and Asleif. Not even Jok. Under the key's power, Zack had always been able to read the written symbols of the Prophecy, and he had often translated them for his tribe.

So Asleif had been sending messages with her birds, back and forth from Lykill. That's how Erik always knew where Jok was headed.

And Zack had never suspected her. He had thought the traitor was a member of Jok's council.

I'm such an idiot.

It all seemed so obvious now.

Why didn't I go to Lykill instead . . . find Jok . . . let him know I'm here? Why did I think I could do this alone?

Monday-morning quarterback. That's what his father would have called him. It was a lot easier to know the right plays once the game was over.

And it's definitely over.

Now Jok might never even find out that Zack had come back. It was too late.

Or was it?

Zack looked back at the birdcage.

What if—

His thoughts were interrupted by a poke in the ribs.

"Lost Boy!"

Ogmunder stood in front of him. As Zack looked up, the wizard blew a handful of powder in his face. Immediately his eyes began to burn. He struggled to free his hands so he could wipe at the stinging tears.

"What did you . . ."

A wave of nausea came on fast. The ground seemed to tilt one way and his stomach went the other. The dim lamplight in the tent seemed to flare brightly, and then everything he saw faded to a light blue haze. He could hear Erik chuckling as the blue darkened to black, and he slipped into unconsciousness.

❧

Zack woke up alone, on the table in Ogmunder's tent. His hands were still tied. A chain around his ankle was secured to the table leg. Daylight showed through the tent flaps. He must have been knocked out all night.

His mouth felt like two pieces of sandpaper stuck together, and his head felt like it was stuffed with cotton. His thoughts came slowly as he remembered what had happened.

Ogmunder . . . Erik . . . Asleif.

Her face passed through his mind like the memory of someone he used to know. But it wasn't going to help to think about her betrayal now. He had to focus on where he was.

A sentry was stationed outside the tent's entrance. Zack stayed still, trying not to draw any attention as he looked around. Shadows on the fabric walls showed him that guards were posted on every side.

His eyes fell on the covered birdcage, and his half-formed idea from the night before came back to him.

What if . . .

If these birds knew the way to Lykill, he might be able to use them to get a message to Jok. Use Erik's own trick against him.

But what kind of message do you send someone who can't read?

What could he send? Yggdrasil's Key, of course, but there was no way Zack could send that.

But maybe the cord?

Jok had given Zack the length of walrus-skin cord that held the key around his neck. But would he recognize it now? It seemed like an incredible long shot.

Yeah, well, a long shot beats no shot at all.

The sentry pushed open the tent flap and looked inside. Zack played dead. He kept his eyes closed until he heard the sentry strike up a conversation with another soldier outside.

Watching the entrance, Zack slipped off the table. The chain around his ankle looked long enough to get him to the edge of the tent. That was all he would need. He held it behind his back to keep it from rattling as he scooted across the dirt floor.

The clay pot Asleif had broken still lay in pieces on the ground. Zack sat with his back to it and managed to pick up one of the larger shards. After a quick bit of manipulation, he was able to start sawing at the rope around his wrists. It quickly gave way. His skin was raw and red where the rope had been, but that was the least of his worries.

Next, he exchanged the walrus-skin cord around his neck

for part of the rope that had tied his hands. He knotted the rope into a loop and put the key on again. Then, with his back to the entrance, he tore off a small piece of the light fabric that covered the birdcage, using his body to block the sound. Then he reached carefully into the cage.

The birds remained docile. They were obviously used to being handled. Zack's fingers closed around one of them. He could feel its heartbeat against his palm.

After he checked once more over his shoulder, he wrapped the cord in the fabric and then tied it in a bundle to the bird's leg with the corners of the cloth.

I hope this is the way they do it.

It seemed crazy that after everything he had been through it should all come down to this—a bird and a piece of string. So far, so good, but would the bird fly to Lykill? And if it did, would Jok understand?

The only thing left was to let the bird go without it being seen. That meant he needed a distraction. Zack took a deep breath.

He reached up and, with one great heave, brought Ogmunder's supply table crashing over on its side. Pots and jars shattered. Powders flew into the air, filling the tent with a thick dust. Dozens of birds and rodents began to shriek.

Zack crouched down next to the tent wall. He waited for the guard on the other side to come running. As soon as the soldier's feet moved away, Zack lifted the tent fabric and thrust the bird outside. It fluttered its wings tentatively.

"Go!" he whispered urgently, and the little bundle lifted out of his hand as the bird took off. At the same moment, a shout came from inside the tent.

"He's trying to escape!"

The chain around Zack's ankle tightened painfully as he was dragged backward across the ground. He yelled out louder than he needed to, hoping to keep as much attention inside the tent as possible and away from the back, where the bird was hopefully on its way.

Zack thrashed against the guards, but it was six against one. By the time the dust began to clear, they had him up on his knees with his hands tied again behind his back. The missing bird went unnoticed in the mess that now littered the tent.

A minute later, Erik came in, followed by Ogmunder.

"What in Odin's name happened in here?" Ogmunder yelled.

Erik turned on the wizard. "You said he would be asleep for two days."

Ogmunder opened and closed his mouth twice before speaking. "It is difficult to make a draught for someone his size. You don't know—"

"No, *you* don't know anything, you dung-spreading, good-for-nothing amateur. I am about done with you."

"I still expect to be paid for my work," Ogmunder said, his voice shaking.

"We'll see about that," Erik said, then turned to the nearest soldier. "Get this camp ready. I want to be in Asgard within three days. Anything later than that and you'll start paying with your men's lives. Do you understand?"

The soldier made a shallow bow. "Yes, sire."

Zack breathed in sharply. Three days to Asgard—the final stop on the quest.

Even if his plan worked, and the bird reached Jok, there was no knowing if Jok would be able to do anything about it before it was too late.

Time was running out.

CHAPTER EIGHT

While the Bears broke camp, Zack was given a small pile of meat rinds and a dipper of water.

"Not too much," Erik had ordered. "Just enough to keep him on his feet. We need him alive."

Zack barely chewed as he gulped all the scraps of food down in a few seconds. The empty, scratching feeling in his stomach was unlike anything he had ever experienced at home. He had been hungry before, but not like this, and never with the worry about when—or if—he would be eating again.

Asleif walked by, carrying a large saddle toward the holding area for the horses. She seemed to be avoiding his gaze as she passed. Zack's pulse quickened. He wanted not to care about her either way, but it wasn't possible to just shake off everything they had been through. If nothing else, he was curious.

"So what happens to you now?" he asked.

Asleif paused in midstride but still didn't look over. "What do you mean?" Her tone was cold and defensive.

"What do you get for all this? What did he promise you?"

Two guards on either side of Zack exchanged a glance. Asleif looked at them and then finally at Zack.

"Why did you do this?" Zack persisted. "What do you owe him?"

"Everything," Asleif blurted out. "He took me in years ago—"

"As his slave," Zack said.

"No," Asleif responded sharply. "Not as his slave."

"What then?" Zack asked. "You do everything he tells you."

"You couldn't understand," Asleif said. "My parents . . . Zack, I watched my parents be killed, before my eyes. I had nothing, no one left, and I would have been killed myself if Erik hadn't taken me in. He saved me, Zack. He cared, when no one else did."

Zack snorted. "So you let him use you to hurt other people, the same way someone hurt your parents?"

Asleif turned toward the horses. The saddle in her arms pushed into Zack and knocked him off the log where he sat. "This is none of your concern," she said, then walked away.

"What do you mean?" Zack yelled from the ground. "You *made* it my concern!"

He would never have imagined he could yell at Asleif about anything. Then again, this wasn't Asleif, at least not the Asleif he knew. This was the person she had been hiding from him all along.

◦⁘◦

Zack's guards lifted him onto the back of a horse behind another soldier and marched on either side as Erik's forces set out. Another heavily guarded horse held Yggdrasil's Chest on its back. Zack hadn't seen the chest since his last trip to the ninth century. Its plain dark wood and iron moldings gave no clue to the chest's famous power, or to the two treasures already sealed inside it.

Scratches and dents in the wood showed where many had tried to break open the chest's three chambers. Fire, swords, axes, and brute human strength were no match for it. The only thing that would open the chest was the key around Zack's neck, which now hung on a conspicuously thick length of rope.

If Erik noticed anything, he didn't let on. He rode next to Zack's horse all morning.

"So you understand that this is all over for you now," Erik said to him after a few hours.

Zack shot back a blank look of contempt. "Nothing's over," he said. No one had to know that the confidence in his voice was resting on a small gray bird, hopefully flying toward Lykill at that moment.

"Well, not exactly over, that's true." Erik jerked his head toward Yggdrasil's Chest. "The best part is yet to come. The end of the quest. The third treasure—Sacrifice, if I'm not mistaken."

"You're an idiot, if I'm not mistaken," Zack muttered to himself.

"There are two ways to win any conflict," Erik went on. "One—stay ahead of your opponent at all times. Or two—

wait until it truly matters, and then profit from his mistakes. When you deserted your tribe, it was more of a mistake than I had ever hoped for."

"I didn't desert them," Zack snapped. He shut his mouth quickly. It was best to tell as little as possible.

Erik looked around as if searching for something. "Well, then I suppose they're somewhere right around here?" When Zack didn't respond, he went on. "Clearly, I can't take that key away from you. But there's nothing to stop me from making sure that you and the key go where I want you to go."

He called out to Asleif, who had been riding at a distance all morning. "Asleif, remind me of the last line of the Prophecy."

"'The way is far, the road will bend, the Boy will lead until the end,'" she called back.

Erik laughed and sat up straighter, then gestured with a gloved hand in the direction they were traveling. "So lead on, Lost Boy."

❧

The rocky vista remained the same all day as they passed from one valley into another. Wherever they were going, it wasn't somewhere you could get to by ship. Zack had never spent so long a time in this world without seeing a river, or lake, or fjord. The only thing marking the dry brown hillsides were dozens of small caves. Their black mouths looked like empty holes punched into the ground.

Zack thought about Minneapolis, and about the snowstorm that had been raging when he left. He imagined all of home as though it were frozen in time at the moment he'd fallen out of the twenty-first century. What would happen if he never fell back in? Was this the part the Free Man had warned him about? If he failed here, did that mean he would never even get to be born?

He wondered about his father, and where all this left Jock Gilman. Would Jock ever know that Zack got erased from history, if that's what happened? Would Jock cease to exist, too? The logic of it was too twisted for any real answers.

By the time they stopped for the night, Zack's mind was as worn out from thinking as his legs were from riding all day without interruption. When two guards pulled him off the back of the horse, he stumbled to a sitting position on the ground. They untied him just long enough to eat. He gulped his meager rations next to the fire as the cool of the night descended.

At dusk, Asleif came over again to where he sat. Zack couldn't tell if the look on her face was softer than before or if it was just the dim light at work.

She stepped in close, and when one of the guards moved toward her, she waved him off dismissively. Zack watched her, curious about what she had to say.

"Lost Boy . . . Zack," she said in a whisper near his ear. "I just want to tell you that none of this was meant to hurt you."

Zack leaned back from her. "What?" It seemed like a crazy thing for her to say.

She went on, even more softly. "For the time I was a part of your tribe, I felt we truly were friends. But that's over now.

And for whatever it's worth, I'm sorry for your trouble."

"Then do something about it," Zack whispered back through clenched teeth.

Asleif stepped away from him. Her expression had hardened again. "That's all I wanted to say," she answered stiffly.

"Yeah, well, congratulations. I hope you feel a lot better." His face was flushed with anger and frustration. There was no reason to believe anything she said anymore, and even if he did, how did it help?

He was still thinking about this as he lay wide-awake that night, looking up at the stars, both exhausted and restless. The rope around his hands and ankles scratched. At least they had tied his hands in front of him so he could lie down. Several Bear soldiers snored all around him on the ground.

The only ones awake besides Zack were the night sentries, two bored-looking guards who paced nearby. The taller of the pair had no front teeth and a black line tattooed across the center of his face. The other guard was squat and stocky, with bulbous muscular arms that stuck out from his body. He had no neck at all. His head sat on his shoulders as though it had been screwed down too tightly.

"How long till this is over?" asked the tattooed guard.

"Dunno," said the other. "Two, three days?"

"And then we get paid? Or then we wait to get paid?"

The short one hawked something up and spit at the fire. "Dunno."

"He's lucky to be the son of Erik the Rich. That much gold buys a lot of loyalty."

"We'll see. I'll count my pay first, decide how loyal I am after."

The tall one grunted his agreement.

Zack rolled back over again, waiting for sleep to come.

He wasn't even aware he had dropped off when a loud screech pulled him awake. It was still dark. The fire nearby was only embers.

Another screech came, echoing off the valley walls. It sounded like a rusty hinge and an angry cat at the same time.

Why is that so familiar?

Torches bounced toward them in the dark.

"Hobgoblins!" someone yelled as they ran past.

That was it. Zack had fought them once before, in Lykill. They were scavengers, and they ate anything—including humans.

Where's Asleif?

By habit, his first thought was of her—of the Asleif he used to know. Then he quickly remembered who she really was. A traitor.

A man's scream cut through the night. Zack heard someone else call out and then the screaming suddenly stopped. A rush of several more sounds reached him—running footsteps, a low rustling, and the crunch of swords into flesh, followed by more high-pitched animal screeching. Somehow the darkness made it harder to know where it was all coming from.

Zack strained against his ropes. "Untie me!" he yelled to the closest guard. The tall one with the tattooed face grabbed him up from the ground. With one swipe of his sword, he freed Zack's feet.

"What about my hands?"

The soldier just took him by the arm in response. "This way."

The short muscular guard stayed with them, walking backward, with a torch in one hand and a sword in the other.

"We need to get out of camp," the tall one said.

"What about Erik?" the other one asked.

"We're to keep the Lost Boy alive," said the tall one. "Erik can worry about himself."

Zack's mind reeled. Was this good for him or bad? Could he get away? Or would it be suicide to try?

Only a few torches in the camp gave some clue to the chaos around them.

Zack looked down the row of tents and saw a pack of hobgoblins run past. They traveled on two feet, but low to the ground like apes. Zack heard more screaming and then the thick, wet sound of flesh being chewed. He did his best to keep from stumbling as the guard pulled him along.

Orn's low voice came from somewhere nearby. "No, no, no, no! Give. Me. That!"

Then he screamed, either in pain or fear, it was hard to tell. Zack suspected he was dead, but a moment later, Orn ran past. He carried a sword and had some kind of blunt object tucked under his arm—Zack realized with a start that it was Orn's other arm. The hobgoblins must have torn it right off.

Orn spat and cursed as he ran. "Ogmunder! Where are you!"

The two guards took Zack to the edge of camp, where several horses were tethered. They whinnied nervously and stamped at the ground.

"What about saddles?" said the muscular guard.

"Forget about them." The tall one pushed Zack toward the nearest horse. "Let's go."

"How am I supposed to get on?" Zack said. He looked one way and then the other, nervously watching for invaders. With his hands tied, he couldn't very well fight them off, much less get onto this horse.

The soldier leaned forward and cupped his hands to give Zack a leg up. "Here."

All at once, the sound of rushing feet came toward them. In the same instant, a hobgoblin landed on the soldier's back with a deafening screech. Zack saw its scaly skin and huge eyes reflected in the torchlight just before he stumbled back and sat down hard on the ground. He scrabbled away backward to get out of range.

The soldier wheeled around in circles, grabbing at the creature. It clung to him with both arms and legs, hugging his torso. "Kill it!"

The other man swung with his sword but missed.

The soldier managed to reach up with his own sword, but the hobgoblin went for his arm as if it were corn on the cob. Zack heard the first bite and then the soldier's howl of pain. He dropped his sword and swung around again to get free.

The shorter soldier stepped in again, wielding his torch this time. It connected with the hobgoblin's head in a shower of sparks. The sword came next. With a quick thrust, he impaled the creature. It went limp and fell dead on the ground.

The tall soldier fell to his knees, clutching his wounded arm. Zack watched from the ground, catching his breath, unsure what to do. In the dim light, he could just see an outline of what was happening. At least one of the horses had broken its tether and run off.

"Can you still ride?" the shorter soldier asked.

The taller one spoke through clenched teeth. "I'll ride. Let's just go."

"Where did those demons come from—"

As if out of nowhere, several more flew at them from the darkness. Zack had been halfway to his feet. Now he jumped back again and stayed low and out of sight. He couldn't see how many hobgoblins there were, but they covered the guards completely.

The two soldiers tried to pluck the hobgoblins off and stabbed at them with their swords. They quickly downed three of the creatures, but several more swarmed over them. The tall soldier reached with his free hand and flung another off his back. To Zack's horror, it flew right toward him. He jumped up but not soon enough. The hobgoblin crashed into him and knocked him flat again. For one sick moment, he looked straight up into the mouth of the creature's long snout. Even in the dark, he could see a row of pointed teeth.

The hobgoblin hissed and reared its head. Zack instinctively put his hands up to his face just as the creature lunged. Its teeth sank into the rope around his wrists. He couldn't see what was happening, but felt the pressure on his arms.

This was his chance. In one swing, he pushed as hard as he could to the side. There was a cracking sound as the hobgoblin's teeth snapped, and the cord on Zack's wrists came loose. With another swing, Zack knocked the hobgoblin away and then jumped to his feet.

The hobgoblin was quick to its feet as well. Zack faced off with it, just long enough to see a thick ooze dripping from its mouth. Then it sprang again.

Zack was ready. He launched forward off the balls of his feet and sacked it in the midsection. The hobgoblin was agile, but Zack outweighed it by at least a hundred pounds. It was like tackling a scarecrow. The hobgoblin flew backward with a screech, rolled across the ground, and scurried away in another direction.

Zack stood panting, with both fists clenched at his sides, ready to run if he had to. He could still hear the sounds of fighting around camp but not nearly as many hobgoblin screeches as before. It sounded as though the Bears had contained the problem.

Several feet away, the taller of his two guards lay still on the ground. The other one was gone. It was exactly the opportunity he needed.

I'm out of here.

He untied the nearest horse, grabbed it by the mane, and pulled himself awkwardly onto its back. The horse didn't need any coaxing. It galloped away the moment Zack was mounted. He leaned forward and hugged its neck, just hoping to stay on.

As he cleared the camp, Zack heard shouting behind him.

"The Lost Boy—"

"Stop him!"

Within a minute, he had passed into the open valley.

He had done it. He had gotten free. His heart soared even as his body pounded up and down like a jackhammer on the back of the galloping horse. He prodded it with his heels to keep going.

It wasn't long before he heard other horses coming from behind and more shouting. He stole a look back but couldn't see anything in the dark. He prodded the horse again.

"Go go go go!"

With a sinking feeling in his gut, Zack realized that he would never be able to outpace the Bears. His only chance of getting away was if he could slip off into the night unnoticed. He looked down at the ground as it raced by in the dark.

Oh man. Not that.

It was going to be like jumping out of a moving car.

All right, don't think about it. Just go.

It had to be soon. He could hear the other riders getting closer.

He leaned as far over to the right side of the horse as he could. Still, he held on tightly. He couldn't yet find the will to do this.

Isn't there something else I can do? Anything? Any—

The decision was made for him. The horse jumped a small ditch and Zack lost his grip.

The first impact was the worst. It was like getting punched in every part of his body, all at the same time. He bounced off the ground once, hit it again, and then rolled several times before coming to a stop.

His hand went to the key—still there. A moment later, he heard the other horses run past.

Zack lay still for several minutes. When he finally did get up, even the groan that escaped him sent a wave of pain through his body.

At some point, the Bears would come back this way. He needed a place to hide, and to rest, and he needed to find it soon.

It didn't take long to find one of the countless caves he had seen on their travels that day. The black circle of its mouth showed faintly in the dark on a nearby hillside. Zack hobbled toward it, each step a reminder of his fall.

Ow. Ow. Ouch. Ow.

The cave was narrow at the opening, but he felt it spread out around him as he crawled inside. Even with the aches and pains in every muscle, it was a great relief to stretch out on the rock floor, completely spent and ready for some undisturbed, much-needed sleep. As he drifted off, he made his plan. He would stay low through the next day and then travel by night. He would do whatever he could to reach Lykill. Everything was back up for grabs. Erik didn't have him or the key anymore. That was what mattered.

He came awake just before dawn. A narrow stripe of sunlight fell into the cave and across his face. Zack rolled over on the hard ground and winced. The soreness was still very much there. Maybe he could go back to sleep for a while.

He put his hands over his ears. The birds were making an amazing amount of noise. Through half-closed eyes, he saw one of them flutter into the cave and land upside down on the ceiling.

Suddenly he came fully awake.

Upside down? On the ceiling?

He stayed still but rolled his eyes to look straight up. The top of the cave was moving. It swayed and chittered. From end to end, it was covered with what looked like a living carpet of . . .

Bats.

Thousands of them, suspended directly overhead. Others continued to fly in from outside, a few at a time. No doubt they were all coming in for a day's sleep after a night of hunting. They probably hadn't been there when Zack fell so soundly asleep.

Okay . . . No sudden moves.

Ignoring the stiffness in his body, he rolled slowly onto his side, then lifted himself up into a crouching position. White splotches of dried bat dung covered the floor. His mouth went sour when he realized he been sleeping on it all night. But that was the least of his worries.

The front of the cave was several yards away—not too far

off, but farther than he would have liked. Before he could make his move, two more bats swooped in from outside. They flew straight toward him. Zack dodged at exactly the wrong moment. One of the bats swerved in the same direction and collided with his head. Tiny sharp claws scratched his scalp and the bat desperately beat its sinewy wings to get free. Zack couldn't help the surprised yell that escaped him, or the storm that it created. In a moment, it felt as though the entire colony of bats had launched off the ceiling. They enveloped him in a squealing, flying cloud.

Small bodies ricocheted off of him. More claws nicked at his scalp and hands. For a moment, Zack was paralyzed with panic. He couldn't see anything but a blur of flying rodents. The mouth of the cave seemed to have disappeared.

Then he dropped to the floor. It wasn't much better. The bats virtually filled the cave from top to bottom. But he did catch sight of his way out. He crawled toward it with one arm over his face. He couldn't see much, but it felt as though the bats were using their sonar to dive-bomb his head, nick at his scalp, and swoop away, one after the other. It nearly stopped him cold.

Finally, a rush of energy—one-half frustration and one-half sheer panic—overtook him. He got to his feet and stumbled headlong through the swarm until he broke free of the cave. He fell forward onto the ground, still waving his arms at bats that were no longer there. A few swooped out of the cave as if to say, *And STAY out!* then swooped back inside.

Zack stood up and leaned against a large rock, waiting for

his nerves to settle. Before they did, however, a voice came across the valley floor.

"There he is!"

Zack looked up and saw several Bear soldiers on horseback. They had probably been looking for him all night.

I guess breakfast and an easy morning is out of the question.

He kicked the ground once in frustration, then took off running. His best bet was straight uphill. Maybe it would be too steep for the horses.

If there was a part of him that wasn't sore, Zack wasn't aware of it, but he pressed on anyway. The slope was covered in flat shale and other rocks that slipped from under his feet. He dug in harder, gaining the slope one painful bound at a time. The Bear soldiers' voices grew closer.

Don't look back.

He looked back. Three of them were directly below him now and starting to climb on foot. Several others were galloping in from farther away.

Zack intensified his effort. As he pulled himself up with his hands, he used his feet to loosen the largest rocks around him. They slid free and cascaded down the hill.

"Watch out!" yelled one of the soldiers. Zack heard another shout out in pain as his voice fell away toward the bottom.

One down, two to go.

He scrambled several yards higher, then scissored his legs over the ground to create another mini-avalanche. A cloud of dust kicked up as it showered over the soldiers, but they held their ground and then kept coming.

Zack looked toward the top of the hill. If he could clear it, he might be able to roll down the other side and get away.

A hand landed on his ankle and pulled. He turned and looked into the face of a scowling blond-bearded soldier.

Resistance fired Zack up. He shook his leg free and, in one automatic motion, caught the soldier flat on the chest with the bottom of his boot. The soldier launched backward and rolled out of control downhill. Another cloud of dust rose up. For a moment, Zack couldn't see anything. He turned to make his escape, but the one remaining soldier dove and grabbed him around the legs. Zack went down.

He struggled to get loose. The soldier tightened his grip, reaching up from behind and wrapping his arm around Zack's chest. Zack couldn't see the man's face, but he could feel their downward movement. They fell as one interlocked body, rolling over each other across the rocks toward the bottom of the slope. By the time they came to a stop, the rest of the Bear patrol had arrived. They jumped off their horses and onto Zack.

Zack breathed heavily through his mouth, his eyes squeezed shut. He had no fight left. The pain in his body, the hunger, the exhaustion were all gone. As the Bears bound him up again and rode him back toward Erik's camp, the only thing he could feel was defeat.

CHAPTER NINE

The post where Zack was tied pressed between his shoulder blades.

Erik stood in front of him, holding his staff in the fire. The carved metal skull he usually used as a torch began to glow orange among the embers. It looked as if it was screaming in pain.

"You've cost me a day," Erik said. "We'll have to find a way for you to pay me back."

Zack now seemed certain where the strangely shaped burn marks on some of the Bear soldiers' faces had come from—like the outline of a skull, scorched into their skin.

"Show him what you mean, sire." Orn bobbed up and down excitedly, swinging an ax in his only hand. A pale yellow lump grew from the shoulder where his arm had once been. Apparently, Ogmunder had begun work on the new one right away.

Others had gathered around as well, including Asleif. Zack could see her through the crowd of Bear soldiers, watching intently from the back.

"Hold this," Erik said. Orn had to drop his ax to take the handle of Erik's staff.

Erik was a full head shorter than Zack and had to look up to meet his gaze when he stepped in close.

"This is no game, Lost Boy. I'm not the kind of fool you think I am."

"Really?" Zack said. "Then what kind of fool are you?"

Erik took a step back and looked down at the glowing metal skull in the fire.

"You are only making the trip to Asgard more unpleasant for yourself."

He took the staff back from Orn and raised the red-hot end toward Zack's face.

"Have you ever smelled a man's burning flesh? It's quite different from the smell of roasting meat. It's sweet almost, not completely unpleasant. Except, of course, for the one whose flesh is burning."

Zack could feel the heat under his chin. He clenched his jaw and tried not to look down. He turned his head and caught Asleif's eye. She stood very still, looking almost frightened. As soon as Zack saw her, she turned and walked away.

"I'm speaking to you!" Erik snapped.

One of the Bear soldiers grabbed Zack's head and turned him to look at Erik. A faint heat vapor rose up between them.

"You've probably guessed that I'm not going to kill you," Erik went on calmly. "But I can make you wish that I had."

The heat came an inch closer. Zack's neck felt as though it was beginning to scorch.

"So tell me, Lost Boy. Are we going to have any further trouble?"

Zack didn't panic, but he knew when to give some ground. He had felt the burn of hot iron once before, in Jok's forge.

"No," he said. His voice was clipped and tight. "Just get that thing away from me."

Erik smiled. "Good. Just so we're clear." He started to lower the staff but then paused and raised it toward Zack's face again. "Maybe just a little something to help you remember."

Zack twisted uselessly against the post at his back. Again, he felt the heat.

"Don't worry," Erik said. "I'll do it quickly."

Suddenly Asleif was there, pushing to the front of the crowd. "Someone's coming!" she yelled.

Erik paused, his eyes still on Zack. "What?"

Asleif came up to him and put a hand on his arm. Erik lowered the hot iron and looked at her.

"One of your scouts," Asleif said. She didn't look at Zack.

A moment later, a soldier on horseback galloped into camp. "Sire! We've spotted the third root of Yggdrasil."

"How far?" Erik demanded.

"A half day's ride," said the soldier.

Erik turned to Zack. "That's good news all around, isn't it?" His eyes darted to the staff. "We'll save this for another time. I want you quick on your feet, Lost Boy." He turned and strode back toward his tent, barking orders to break camp. Zack waited until Erik wasn't looking before he exhaled heavily with a sigh of relief.

He looked around for Asleif, but she had slipped away again. Was he imagining things, or had she just run interference for him? There was no chance to find out. When they left the valley, Asleif kept to herself and avoided Zack's gaze as much as ever.

Erik's scouts led them over a series of pointed hills, steep on the way up and even steeper on the way down. Zack had his own horse this time, but it was chained in a group of three to keep him from breaking away. Several other soldiers rode all around him like a presidential guard. It gave Zack an odd sense of importance. He had never been such a threat to anyone at home. Not even close.

Slowly, Yggdrasil's root came into view. It stretched across the land like an unbroken mountain range. Even from miles away, the deep ruts in its bark were easy to see. Where the root wound out of sight, it merged with an actual mountain, forming one-half of a giant peak that disappeared up into a high line of clouds and fog. It was impossible to see what lay above the cloud line, but Zack suspected he knew. The Norse mythology books he read at home spoke of Bifrost, the Rainbow Bridge leading from Midgard to Asgard, from the world of humans to the home of the gods. The third root of Yggdrasil was said to lead most of the way to Asgard, and Bifrost was said to finish the journey.

The mythology books at home did no justice to the real

thing. Every time Zack saw a part of Yggdrasil, he was reminded how unimaginably huge the whole tree must be. This was just one root, and it was larger than any single thing he had ever seen in the twenty-first century. It would have dwarfed the Metrodome.

I wish Dad could at least just see this.

With all the quest's confusing turns, one thing had grown consistently clearer. Zack wished he had shared more of it with the people from home. At first, it was mostly Ollie and Ashley Williams he thought about. But more and more, Zack realized, his father was on his mind. Maybe that was because he had started to confront an ugly thought—that he might fail at this quest; that he might never get home again; and worst of all, that he might get stuck here somehow and never even be born. The Free Man hadn't said as much, but he'd definitely made it sound like a possibility. To Zack, the idea that his father might never even know him was the most painful prospect of all. As they grew closer to Yggdrasil's root, he silently vowed to do everything he could to keep that from happening. He wasn't going to give up yet. Not until it was over.

Whenever that is. How do you know when you've been erased from history?

With less than a mile to go, Erik halted the company. He ordered all those on horseback to ride ahead with him. Zack estimated it would be a party of two dozen, including Asleif and Ogmunder. Orn, who normally rode, was on foot today.

"We will ride to the Well of Urd," Erik announced to the group. "Orn, I'll expect you to bring the others along quickly. Don't keep me waiting."

Orn nodded curtly. "I'm not accustomed to marching," he said under his breath.

"Well, then maybe I should relieve you of your legs," Erik spat back. Orn looked up at him with seething yellow eyes, but stayed silent.

They set off at a faster pace. The giant tree root loomed ever larger as they came toward the foot of the strange double mountain, half of it earth and rock, the other half brown rutted bark. Zack had hoped that getting to this point would be a cause for celebration. Now it was just the opposite. For all he knew, Lykill was hundreds of miles away. If Jok and the tribe were coming, they were going to arrive too late to salvage the quest.

At the base of the mountain, Erik's party came to a vast crater of some kind. It was roughly circular, like a natural stadium dug into the ground. Inside, it held a scene of such peaceful beauty that Zack wondered if he was seeing things.

Where the ground sloped down and inward, dry earth gave way to lush meadow, as green as AstroTurf. The grass was dotted with orange and yellow wildflowers. At the bottom lay a vast area of flat ground. Two swans swam on a glassy pond, fed by a winding stream. A single tree, heavy with yellow fruit, grew nearby. And under the tree were three women in pale blue-and-green robes.

The arrival of Erik's group was impossible to ignore, but

the women did not look up. One of them continued feeding the swans from a pouch at her side. The other two sat in the shade.

Zack blinked several times. "Is this the Well of Urd?" he whispered. He hadn't intended to speak, but his curiosity got the best of him.

The soldier at his right nodded. "The meeting place of the gods," he whispered back. Even he seemed to be in awe.

"Who are those women?" Zack asked.

"The Norns," said the soldier.

"Norns?"

"The three fates," the soldier answered. "Even the gods bow to their influence."

This was the closest thing to a normal conversation Zack had had since Erik had taken him captive. Everyone had become strangely docile. He wondered if he could use the situation to his advantage, but he was still surrounded by guards.

Erik dismounted and began leading his men down the slope. The ground was soft underfoot, almost spongy. Sounds became muted, and motions seemed to slow down, as though the air was getting thicker. Zack had experienced this once before, when the Free Man had led him toward Yggdrasil for the first time.

They stopped at the bottom of the crater, across the pool from the three women. One of them sat on a gilded bench in the shade of the fruit tree, weaving at a small loom. Another leaned against the base of the tree and read from an unfurled scroll on her lap. The one feeding the swans was closest to them, but none looked up. Their pastel robes moved like water in the soft breeze.

Zack was amazed to see Erik bow deeply to the women and then kneel in the grass. Two soldiers pulled Zack down as everyone else knelt, too.

"I bring you the blessings of Midgard," Erik said, in a voice far gentler than Zack had ever heard from him.

The woman at the loom stopped her work and stood up. She came to the edge of the pool. Her face was drawn and wrinkled, but she stood erect and her movements were fluid. She stared at Erik, then at Zack and the others.

Zack knew he had nothing to lose.

"Who are you?" he asked. His voice felt muted in the strange atmosphere.

Erik looked over at him but didn't say anything.

The older woman bowed her head. "I am Urd. These are my sisters, Verdandi and Skuld." She motioned to the two much younger women. Both looked up for the first time. The one feeding the swans, Verdandi, gave a knowing smile. Skuld's expression was much darker. She rolled her scroll and clutched it against her chest. The two of them came and stood next to Urd.

Erik spoke again. "We come bearing Yggdrasil's Key and Yggdrasil's Chest. We have also brought the Lost Boy. He is ready for his fate."

"Yes, I know," said Urd.

Zack stood up. "I'm not here by choice." It felt like a

shout in his throat, but the words came out softly. He pointed at Erik. "He stole the chest from my tribe."

To Zack's surprise, no one responded. The three women watched and listened without emotion. Erik and his soldiers stayed on their knees, until Zack turned to go. Then two Bears stood up and drew their swords to block his way.

"Help me get out of here," Zack tried to yell. "This is wrong." The softness of his words doubled his frustration. It was like a bad dream.

Finally, Urd spoke. "We are not concerned with right and wrong, but with past, present, and future."

"But—"

"I know that you are the Lost Boy and that you carry Yggdrasil's Key. It is through you that Yggdrasil's Chest has realized two of its three treasures."

Zack pointed to Erik. "And now he's stealing them. They don't belong to him."

"Nor do they belong to you," said Urd calmly. "Nor to anyone else. The only thing that belongs to you is your fate. And your fate is nothing more than your future becoming your past." She stared at him, quizzically examining his face. "I see you have come a long way on this quest, but the rest of your past is a blur to me."

"That's because—" Zack stopped himself from finishing. *That's because I'm from the future.*

"And now here you are," said Verdandi. She spoke in a clear, lilting voice.

"Only 'cause they're forcing me," Zack called out. He pushed against the soldiers' crossed swords, but they held their ground.

Verdandi nodded and then went on as if Zack hadn't spoken. "Know this: Yggdrasil's Key and Yggdrasil's Chest may be carried by one each, or by one alone. Only those who bear them may enter the gates of Asgard, where the third treasure waits."

"Can I stop this from happening?" Zack asked. He impulsively looked at Erik, but Erik seemed as unconcerned as ever, intent only on what the women were saying.

"That is not a question for me," Verdandi said, looking back at Skuld.

Skuld clutched her scroll more tightly. "I cannot know what you are capable of doing, Lost Boy. I deal only with what will happen."

Zack sighed. "What's going to happen, then?"

"That, I will not tell you. Your fate is for you to find. But I will tell you this: Even the tree Yggdrasil will decay and die"—she motioned to the vast tree root, which loomed above the crater—"there is no escaping the ends of things. Your choice is only in how you will meet the ends that find you." She drew a veil across her face and turned away.

"Wait!" called Zack. He shook with frustration.

"May we pass?" Erik asked.

Urd nodded. "You may." At that, the three women returned to their work and did not look up again.

Erik grinned broadly at Zack. "It's time for us to move on."

Back at the top of the slope, Orn and the rest of the Bears had arrived. Most of them sat or lay on the ground, recovering from what must have been a long run to catch up. Zack felt the air and the sounds around him return to normal.

"On your feet!" Erik yelled, his voice back to its usual whine. As the soldiers stood up, he mounted his horse, which was the only place where he could be taller than everyone. He addressed them from there, his words dripping with self-importance.

"We are beginning the last leg of our journey toward Asgard, where I will cross the Bifrost Bridge with the Lost Boy, claim the final treasure, which is my right, and reap the reward of the gods."

"And then . . . ?" asked Ogmunder.

"Yes, yes, yes," growled Erik. "Then you will all be paid your wage." He kicked his horse in the side and cantered uphill. The Bears let out a cheer and began following Erik up the mountain.

Zack stayed vigilant as the soldiers compelled his horse along. He searched his mind for some idea, some last chance. Could Erik really force him to cross the Bifrost Bridge into Asgard? Was there any way to turn this around? And what would it mean for Jok and everyone in Lykill if Erik succeeded?

I don't know, I don't know, I don't know.

It was like pounding his head against a door that wouldn't open. Despite everything he had accomplished, it had all come to this.

They rode for several hundred yards but then had to abandon the horses as the mountain grew steeper. One of the guards pulled Zack to the ground, and another tied his hands behind his back once again. They marched on in a tight formation around him, with a knot of soldiers guarding Yggdrasil's Chest. It went on this way for an hour or more.

Wisps of fog blew down around them as they approached the cloud line. The rest of the mountain was shielded from view, but through the mist Zack began to see three bright bands of color—red, green, and blue—receding into the distance. The Bifrost Bridge. It was impossible to tell through the clouds, but it seemed to be made entirely of light. At the sight of it, Zack's heart sank the rest of the way to rock bottom. It wasn't supposed to end this way.

"There it is," Erik said with a gloating tone. "Our last crossing."

He had barely spoken the words when a soft rumbling came through the ground. Zack felt it in his feet like an earthquake. *Avalanche,* he thought. But then he heard a voice. It came from up the slope, somewhere in the clouds above them. It was a single, booming roar. Then several other voices joined in, and the sound grew until it was one enormous howl.

Not a howl, but something more familiar. A battle cry.

Erik looked sharply at Zack, as if he was supposed to do something about it. The Bear soldiers glanced around from one to the other.

The roar grew louder. Zack heard pounding feet and the rattle of chain mail just before he saw where it was all coming from.

Jok was leading the charge, alongside the warrior sisters Hilda and Helga. The combined forces of their two tribes ran behind them, streaming out of the fog in a full-on ambush.

CHAPTER TEN

They might as well have been an avalanche. Jok, Hilda, Helga, and their tribes ran down the slope like an unstoppable wave. In the center of the pack, someone carried a familiar yellow-and-white diamond-patterned banner. The sight of it filled Zack with a rush of confidence—something like the "purple pride" his father always talked about. He felt like an empty tire suddenly inflated with air as he watched them attack.

Jok wore a steel helmet with a mask that came down over his nose and eyes. He carried a round wooden shield and his sword, Lightning. His ax, called Thunder, hung at the ready, over his back.

Hilda and Helga carried their own finely gilded swords and wore long coats of nickel-colored chain mail. As the charge drew near, they pulled away from Jok and led a separate faction to attack the Bears from two sides.

The Bears sprang into action and charged up to meet them. In a moment, the mountainside rang with the clash of metal as the battle began.

The soldiers around Zack pressed in close. They blocked his view of the fighting, and pulled him and Yggdrasil's Chest to the rear.

Zack shouted out, "Jok!" but the battle sounds drowned

him out. He tried to twist away from the two soldiers who pulled him along. With his hands tied behind his back, he couldn't exert enough strength.

Suddenly Erik was next to Zack. He pushed in like a puppy looking for the warm spot in the litter.

"To the bridge!" he yelled. He barked orders for them to go around, skirting the battle in the direction of the Bifrost Bridge. Its bright colors showed the way through the clouds. Zack dragged his feet as they pushed toward it.

"Let them all kill each other," Erik muttered. "It just means fewer men for me to pay."

The Bear soldiers on Zack's left held their shields closely together to form a wall on the battle side, protecting them from flying arrows and keeping Zack out of sight. Zack craned his neck, trying to get someone's—anyone's—attention as they circled around the fighting.

He caught sight of Hilda and Helga, working in unison. One of them swung with her sword while the other caught an attacker at the legs. A Bear soldier went down, and they stepped forward to meet the next one. Neither of them noticed Zack as he was dragged along.

The red, green, and blue of the bridge grew more vivid as they came closer to it. Where it connected with the mist, it sent small bursts of color in every direction, like a prism.

Zack looked across the mountain slope and saw Sven fighting next to Lars. Their faces were mostly obscured under their helmets and faceplates, but Sven's silver hair, and Lars's tall thin frame, were unmistakable. And next to them was a tall female fighter. Her face was hard to see, but the bushy auburn hair could only have belonged to one person.

Valdis!

She had always stayed home before, and now Zack wondered why. She fought like a seasoned warrior, swinging twin hammers, one in each hand, with amazing precision. As Bears came toward her, she managed to keep them at bay with one hammer, and swing far enough with the other to knock them off their feet. Zack couldn't help laughing out loud, even in the midst of the danger. It made perfect sense that his sister's double could be this dangerous.

Valdis paused and looked in Zack's direction. For a brief second, their eyes met.

"Hey!" Zack strained against the rope on his wrists. He tried to jump up to be seen.

"Keep him under control," Erik ordered.

One of the soldiers clapped a studded glove onto the top of Zack's head. It felt like a falling brick. Zack groaned and shut his eyes against the pain.

And then something plowed into them like a Mack truck. Zack went flying to the side. Bear soldiers fell like bowling pins. He saw Erik and Yggdrasil's Chest tumble in the other direction. For a moment, everything was confusion.

Valdis was there, with Harald, Sigurd, and a dozen of their tribe mates. Zack's head reeled with pain and excitement as he watched Harald and Sigurd seize the chest. They started backing up with it, brandishing their swords. Valdis covered them, her hammers flying. Erik screamed orders, but the Bears around him had their hands full with the attack.

Zack jumped up and tried to run, but two Bear soldiers tackled him before he could take a step. Valdis glanced over, wild-eyed.

"Lost Boy!" she shouted, but she couldn't get to him through the wall of fighting around her.

"Don't lose him!" Erik screamed frantically from somewhere else, and then, "The chest! The chest!" Zack couldn't even see him anymore through all the bodies.

The two guards holding Zack grunted in pain, one after the other. They loosened their grip on his arms and fell away. Zack twisted around to see. At first it seemed no one was there except for the two guards who lay writhing on the ground, clutching at wounds on their legs.

"Is best to keep still," said a familiar voice.

Zack looked down. "Olaf!" He nearly burst with happiness to see his friend.

Olaf held a short dagger to the ropes around Zack's wrists. With a quick slice, he cut them loose. Zack grabbed him by the shoulders and shook his hand, momentarily forgetting where he was.

"I didn't even see you coming!" he said with a laugh.

"Is good to be small sometimes," Olaf told him, beaming. The red dots of his eyes shone brightly, and he gave Zack a quick hug. "Now is time to be going."

Zack felt ready for anything. "Which way?"

One of the downed soldiers reached out from the ground and grabbed Zack's ankle. Zack went down but then kicked away from the Bear's grasp and scrambled uphill, out of reach. The soldier tried to stand up but then fell back down.

Olaf stood ready with his dagger. He held it to the soldier's neck and pulled off the man's bear cloak, then threw it to Zack.

"Is better to not be seen as Lost Boy," he said. "Go. Find Jok."

Zack put the cloak on and pulled the hood over his head. He figured that he and Olaf shouldn't be seen together now. "Which way?"

Olaf pointed. "Go!"

"I'll see you soon."

Zack ran in the direction Valdis and the others had taken the chest. He held the cloak tightly around him, knowing there was a risk of being attacked by one of his own tribe mates. But it was the only way to hide on the battlefield.

Soon he saw his friends, running with the chest. Beyond them, Jok was clustered with Hilda, Helga, and several others. Zack ran the long way around toward them. When he was nearly there, Jok turned and saw him. His eyes grew wide and he charged, raising his sword.

"JOK!" Zack yelled. He threw off the cloak, and Jok stopped just a few feet from him.

"Zack!" Jok reached for him, and grabbed his shoulders. He shook Zack violently, with adrenaline-fed joy. "It's done!" he yelled. "You're here!"

An instant later, Jok turned back to where Harald and Sigurd were running toward them with the chest. He motioned for them to charge direction. They seemed to know exactly what to do. They dropped the chest next to Hilda and Helga, then led a full reverse charge at the Bears who had been coming after them.

Zack heard another battle within the battle break out as Harald and the others created a cover for him and Jok.

"Now's our time!" Jok yelled. He took Zack by the arm and hustled him up to where the twins guarded the chest. Without stopping, they each took a handle on one side of it and ran for the bridge. The twins traveled with them, guarding their backs.

"Thanks for coming!" Zack yelled. He felt almost giddy with this turn of events.

"You're welcome," Jok shouted back with a grin.

The bridge looked like a swirl of colored gas up close. When Zack stepped onto it, he felt a tingle in his feet. It was like standing on colored air, but it supported his weight as if it were made of rock. The prismatic glints of red, green, and blue that shot off the surface were bright as neon.

Jok stopped and set down his side of the chest.

Zack turned to look at him and the twins. All three stood on the mountain ground while he was already standing on the bridge. "What are you doing?" he asked.

"Zack, you have to keep going now. Don't stop," Jok said.

"Where are you going?" He couldn't believe Jok would turn back now, so soon after they had found each other.

"This isn't over yet," Jok said. He pointed toward the battle. "They need our help."

There was no time for anything. And somehow, as Zack looked up at Jok, he realized something.

It was like unscrambling a code. Finally, it made sense.

"You knew," he said. "You knew about Asleif, didn't you? That's why you left her there with Erik before."

Jok gave a sharp nod. "I suspected as much. Now go. Finish this."

Without another pause, he turned and followed the twins back toward the fighting.

Zack steeled himself for the final run. He grasped the handle on the side of the chest and dragged it along behind him.

The bridge stretched away from the mountainside, over a cloud-filled void. Zack could see through the translucent color at his feet to the clouds maybe fifty yards below. Whatever lay beyond that was a mystery.

The bridge had no railing and was about ten feet across. Zack stuck to the center. At the far end, in the distance, he could see the outer wall of Asgard. It sat on a vast plateau that floated like a huge island in the sky.

The main wall stood as straight and tall as any man-made structure, but several wild-looking waterfalls cascaded down the front of it, into a wide silvery river that ran like a moat around the city. The colored bands of the Bifrost Bridge led right onto the plateau, over the river, and ended at a high arched gate.

Beyond the wall was Asgard itself. It looked like a small city superimposed on the image of a mighty forest. Most of

Asgard's towers rose straight into the air, then spread out at the top like great stone oaks. They were capped with turrets in shades of gold, copper, and silver that caught the sun. Zack stood at the peak of the bridge, awed by the sight of it.

Suddenly the ground vibrated underfoot. He looked down. It came in a series of soft beats—it was the even rhythm of running steps, he suddenly realized.

He turned just in time to see Erik coming at him, with Asleif not far behind.

Erik caught him off guard and knocked him down. The chest fell on its side. A moment later, Erik was on top of him, but Zack flipped him off and rolled away.

Erik stood up, panting. "We can cross into Asgard together," he said. "But I'll kill you before I let you go alone." He produced a sword from under his cape.

Zack's fists clenched. He hadn't even thought to ask Jok for a weapon.

"Erik!" Asleif yelled, running to catch up.

"Stay back," Erik told her. He kept his gaze and his sword toward Zack.

Zack looked from Erik to Asleif, to the chest, which lay precariously near the edge of the bridge. Back on the mountainside, it sounded as though the battle was still on, but the fog and clouds blocked Zack's view. That meant Jok would have no way of seeing he was in trouble.

"Let's just take the chest and go," Asleif said. "The Lost Boy doesn't have to die."

"I know that, you idiot," Erik snapped. "I need him. He has to come with me."

"What about me?" she asked.

"What about you?"

"I thought—"

Erik whipped around and slapped her in the face. Asleif staggered several steps away. Zack reached for Erik, but his sword kept him at bay.

"You obviously don't know where your loyalties lie," Erik seethed. "Take your weak sympathy and go, before I run you through." He waved the sword toward her, and Zack seized his chance. With reflexes he didn't even know he had, he was on Erik in a flash.

As they went down, Erik swung once with his sword. It whizzed through the air. Zack felt a line of pain cross his forearm and he reeled back. From the ground, Erik swung again. In a moment of blind panic, Zack saw the blade coming right for his face.

Asleif was there again. She grabbed Erik's wrist in midair, then wrenched his arm backward at the elbow. Erik yelled out and dropped the sword. It bounced off the bridge with an electric twanging sound, and fell noiselessly down into the void below.

Erik tried to hit Asleif with his good arm, but again, she blocked him and pushed back hard. The force of it sent him toward the edge of the bridge. His eyes flew wide open as he realized he was going over. He reached out and connected with Asleif's leg. She jerked forward. Erik disappeared off the bridge and Asleif went with him.

Zack dove. He locked hands with Asleif as she fell, then landed flat against the bridge on his stomach. "I've got you," he yelled.

Asleif dangled by one arm over the void with Erik hanging on to her legs below. She was silent, but the terror in her eyes was clear. Zack grabbed her other arm and got a better grip, but her weight combined with Erik's was nearly too much.

Don't. Let. Go.

Whatever had happened between them didn't matter right now. He had to hold on. The pulse in his head throbbed with the effort. His arms felt like two bolts of white-hot pain and it was all he could do just to stay where he was.

Erik grunted and managed to get a higher grip on Asleif's body. He was actually starting to climb up her. Zack felt himself slide an inch closer to the edge.

"Don't!" he grunted, trying to conserve his strength. He couldn't even afford the energy of being afraid. He focused on Asleif's face.

"Zack," she said weakly.

Erik pulled himself up again and Zack slid forward. His chest came off the bridge. He looked down and saw Erik's expression, somewhere between fear and insanity.

"Zack," Asleif said again, almost in a whisper. "I'm sorry." She twisted her arms, trying to get loose.

Zack found the strength to yell out.

"No!"

His muscles shook as his panic began to take over.

Erik was on Asleif's back now. He reached for Zack's arm, maybe to pull himself up, or maybe to pull Zack off, there was no knowing which.

Asleif grunted once more and, with a sudden intensity, wrenched herself free.

Zack's empty hands flew back. An overwhelming helplessness suddenly took the place of his panic. He saw Asleif and Erik fall, their gaping mouths making a noise he couldn't hear. They slipped through the air, almost gracefully. Before they were too small to see, they passed through the layer of white clouds and were gone.

CHAPTER ELEVEN

They were already gone, but Zack couldn't bear to look into the void. He pulled away and shut his eyes. For all he knew, Erik and Asleif were still falling.

It didn't feel real. It had happened too quickly. Just like that, Erik was out of the equation.

And Asleif was gone.

Zack lay still on the bridge, trying to make sense of it. He couldn't shake the feeling that he had just lost a friend. Asleif had caused his tribe so much trouble along the way, but she just saved his life with her sacrifice.

The word rolled over in his mind and stuck there.

Sacrifice.

The third treasure. The reason he was here, on this bridge. The reason he had to stand up and keep going. If he didn't, it was all for nothing.

He got slowly to his feet. Once again, he lifted the end of the chest and dragged it toward Asgard.

This wasn't what he thought the end of the quest would be. He had come all this way, and still he felt alone. He *was* alone. It was a strange and unexpectedly hollow feeling.

As he drew toward the main gate, Zack saw that it was wrought iron, flecked with gold, forged to look like a lattice of leaves and twisting branches. He recognized the pattern right away. It was a gigantic version of the same shapes carved into Yggdrasil's Key.

A single guard stood in front of the gate. The walls of Asgard were so high, it was difficult to gauge the man's height. He looked at least ten feet tall. Instead of a sword, he wore a long curved horn on a plain leather strap at his side. When he smiled in Zack's direction, the sun reflected back a mouthful of gold teeth. His broad hand, held up in greeting, looked like it could palm a watermelon. Zack approached him tentatively. Things here were not always what they seemed.

"The battle has ended," said the guard, pointing back the way Zack had come.

Zack looked, but all he saw was clouds and the empty Bifrost Bridge. "How do you know?" he asked.

The guard winced and put his hands over his ears. "No need for shouting."

Zack's confusion doubled. "Um . . . How do you know the battle's over?" he whispered.

"I am Heimdall." the guard said, as though it explained everything.

The name was unfamiliar. "I'm sorry," Zack said softly. "I don't really—"

"Guardian of Asgard," Heimdall went on proudly. "The name may not be familiar, but certainly you've heard tell of my eyes and ears?"

Luckily, Zack didn't have to answer. Heimdall barely took a breath, then kept going.

"My sight and my hearing are unparalleled in all the nine worlds. Not to boast, but I can hear wool growing on sheep, and see for over a hundred miles." He paused now, and reached up to smooth the two long braids on either side of his head.

"Uh . . . wow. That's amazing," Zack said, giving him the reaction he seemed to be waiting for. Then he asked, "So can you tell me what's happening over there now?"

"There is shouting, but no more swordplay. The fighting has stopped."

All Zack heard was wind.

"Who won?" he asked eagerly.

Again, Heimdall winced. "Do you mind?"

"Sorry. Who won?" he said, trying to contain himself.

"Those who fought for the red-haired man," Heimdall said, and Zack's heart soared.

He pumped both fists in the air. "Yes!" he said, keeping it to a strong whisper.

"The ones with the dark cloaks have given up. They are leaving the mountain," Heimdall told him.

"That's because they're not getting paid," Zack said with a grin. "They're soldiers for hire."

"How human," Heimdall said, wrinkling his nose.

"What about the ogre?" Zack asked. "Do you see the one all covered in fur?"

Heimdall looked again. "With a single arm?"

"Yeah, that's him."

"He and the wizard were the first ones to leave."

Zack's breath sped up. "And what about the others? My tribe?" he asked quickly. "Where are they?"

Heimdall squinted toward the glowing bridge and nodded. "They are on their way."

Zack looked back again, but still saw little more than the white void. The image of Asleif falling through the clouds came painfully back into his mind.

"How far down does that go?" he asked, not sure he wanted to know.

"It depends," said Heimdall. "It leads to many places. The landing is soft enough, but the way out may be difficult."

"What do you mean?"

"The two who fell may find themselves in the world of the light elves, if they're lucky. Or perhaps the dwarves, or the dark elves, if they're not."

"Do you mean they're not—"

"Dead? That's unlikely." Heimdall looked again toward the bridge. "But if they wish to get back to Midgard, it will be a difficult trip."

Zack squeezed his eyes shut. He felt as though he were trying to file away too much information at once. Erik and Asleif were alive—somewhere. The Bears were gone. Most importantly, Jok and the others were safe and on their way over.

Heimdall prodded Zack. "I see you have the chest with you, and I assume you carry Yggdrasil's Key as well?"

Zack took out the key and showed it to him. Heimdall immediately lifted his horn and blew a single, long, clear note.

The iron branches carved into the enormous gate suddenly came alive. They twisted away from each other, opening like a zipper down the center, and the two sides swung slowly open.

Zack watched it, slack-jawed.

"The gates of Asgard never remain open for long," Heimdall told him.

Zack looked inside and then back to the bridge several times quickly. "I want to wait for my tribe," he said.

Already the gate had begun to swing closed.

"Only those who bear Yggdrasil's Chest and Yggdrasil's Key are to be admitted," Heimdall reminded him.

It was frustrating to have to go in alone, but Zack knew what he had to do. He quickly pulled the chest inside and the iron gate shut behind him with an echoing clang.

"Good luck, Lost Boy."

Zack was surprised to see Heimdall standing right behind him. Without another word, he brushed past and marched to the far side of the wide courtyard. The ground, Zack saw, was paved with tiles of all different sizes. Some seemed to be made of wood; others were stone. One nearest Zack was transparent, like a window in the ground. He could see through to a pool, where several dozen brightly colored fish swam back and forth.

When he looked up again, Heimdall passed through a doorway at the far side of the courtyard. It was blocked by a waterfall, which stopped just long enough to let him through, then continued flowing.

The towers of Asgard were indeed like trees—similar to one another in shape, but each one with its own flourishes and unique qualities. Some were enormously tall, like redwoods. The highest one Zack could see was made of a silvery-white stone and covered in miles of dark green ivy. Where it flared at the top, he could just make out a gleaming gold dome, with a jet of water that burst like a geyser from the peak. The water ran down the gold roof and fell hundreds of feet like heavy rain to the ground.

Long staircases and suspended walkways cut the sky in every direction, connecting one tower to another. Some ran sharply up and down, while others curved lazily between short clusters of copper-roofed buildings.

Across the courtyard, Zack noticed that a small crowd had gathered on one of the stone walkways high above. As he watched, Heimdall came through a doorway on the side of a nearby tower and joined the others. They all looked human, but taller.

At the end of the row, next to a white-bearded man, Zack saw Huginn and Muninn perched on the wall. It was a surprise to see them, until he remembered that Asgard was their home.

He ran toward them, awkwardly pulling the chest behind him. One of the ravens ruffled its wings, but the bearded one put out a hand and the raven grew still.

Zack now saw that another figure among them was familiar. He stood apart from the others with his hands clasped behind his back. He stared down from above, and something about his manner, even from this distance, told Zack not to go any closer. His wild red hair and beard reminded him of his father, and of Jok.

As Zack came to the middle of the courtyard, the key around his neck stirred. He felt a soft, but familiar, vibration against his chest. When he took the key out, it was glowing faintly as if from the inside.

A warm excitement stirred in his gut.

This is it.

Yggdrasil's Key glowed only for one thing.

Sacrifice was somewhere nearby.

Zack took the key off and held it out in front of him. If the first two treasures were any indication, the glow and the vibration would get stronger as he got closer to Sacrifice. He scanned the courtyard. What kind of treasure would it be?

"Lost Boy!"

Zack turned and saw the one thing that could add to his excitement. Jok and the rest of the tribe stood pressed against Asgard's gate. They cheered as he ran toward them.

Jok reached between the wrought-iron branches and shook Zack's forearm with both his hands. His leather tunic was torn down the front, and a long cut ran down the length of his cheek.

"You're alive!" Zack yelled.

"What did you expect?" Jok said.

Zack looked from one blood- and dirt-streaked face to the next. Valdis stood next to Jok, with Harald, Lars, Sven, Sigurd, and the twin sisters crowded around.

"Where's Olaf?" he asked urgently, almost choking on the question. Then he saw a familiar pair of pointed ears pushing toward the front.

"Is right here!" he yelled. He reached up and grabbed Zack's hand.

"Did we lose anyone?" Zack asked.

"Some," Helga answered darkly. "They'll be remembered, but they fell so near to Asgard, their journey to Valhalla won't be far." Everyone cheered again.

"Now go finish this, Lost Boy," said Valdis, as friendly as she had ever been. She had a purple welt above her eye, but smiled warmly.

"Valdis, I'm glad you're here," Zack said honestly.

"I wasn't going to be left behind," she said. "Not again."

Sven reached out and tussled her head. "We couldn't stop her this time."

"You want to keep that hand?" Valdis snapped at him.

Zack laughed. This was the Valdis he was used to.

"Now go," Jok ordered.

Zack put his hands up against the enormous gate, wishing it to open.

"You have to do this," Jok said. "Go."

Zack turned away reluctantly and, once again, held the key out in front of him. He followed its vibration toward the far left corner of the courtyard. He expected it to lead him through one of the many doorways, but soon found that he was headed straight for a solid wall. A soft glow showed around the edges of one stone in particular.

There it is.

He forced himself to breathe slowly, keeping his focus. It wasn't over yet.

For one thing, how was he going to get through the wall without any tools? As he stepped up to it, the vibrating intensified. He could hear a single high-pitched note humming inside his head. The glow from behind the wall seemed to take over the stone itself, which was now a large square of brilliant golden light. The key matched its intensity and Zack had to squint to see.

The treasure wasn't behind the wall. It was right here in front of him.

Sacrifice is a piece of stone?

He reached up to touch it, and immediately everything cooled. The golden light dimmed back to a soft glow, and the humming in Zack's head subsided.

Okay. Now what?

He didn't have to get through the wall, but he did still have to loosen the stone somehow. It was the size of a small rectangular tabletop, and a plain sandy color like the rest of the wall. A border of mortar held it firmly in place.

Zack was suddenly aware of the pounding silence. He had nearly forgotten all the eyes on him, but now turned to see. His tribe was still pressed eagerly against the gate. Jok had both hands on the bars, like someone in a jail cell. No one spoke.

He looked up at the others, the ones who stood high above, staring imperiously down at him.

"A little help?" Zack asked halfheartedly. This was Asgard after all. If the gods couldn't lend a hand, who could? But none of them raised so much as an eyebrow. The one with the red hair and beard crossed his huge arms over his chest and pulled down the corners of his mouth.

Looks like someone woke up on the wrong side of the cloud this morning.

He smiled at his own joke, but it only seemed to make the guy grouchier. Zack turned back to his work.

Okay, so it's going to be a solo job. Nothing like a little pressure.

He fought to concentrate. The stone offered no clue. When he scratched at the mortar, it scraped like sandpaper against his finger. A few bits of dust came loose but nothing that made a difference. He would grind a hundred fingers down to stubs trying to do this by hand.

He started to put the key back around his neck so he could use both hands. Then he paused.

He looked down at it, at the three key stems that opened the chambers of the chest. Each one was hard metal—the closest thing to a tool he could imagine.

Am I allowed to . . . ?

He held the key up to the wall, wondering if anyone would stop him. Still, no one stirred. He scratched again at the mortar, and this time, a much heavier amount of dust gave way.

"Yes!" he shouted out loud, his heart picking up speed.

He scraped harder, and faster. The work was quick, and the mortar crumbled under the force of the key. Zack's focus narrowed. All he saw now was the key scraping against the wall. All he knew was that he wasn't going to stop until he was done.

He scraped back and forth, back and forth, working on one side of the stone, then the other. Sweat rolled into his eyes but he barely noticed. He lost all sense of time. It might have been an hour later, but all of a sudden the stone tilted a fraction of an inch. It broke whatever trance Zack had been in, and he jumped back in surprise.

He pried at the edge of the stone with his fingers. It pulled away another tiny bit, then stuck again. More determined than ever, Zack put the key back on, bit down hard, and braced his foot against the wall. He pulled the stone with both hands. His muscles strained. The tendons in his neck felt like they would pop. And then, with a soft scrape, the stone pulled free. It fell with a heavy thud, facedown onto the ground.

He heard another cheer from the gate, where everyone was watching.

Behind the stone was an empty gap in the wall, nothing more than bits of mortar, and more rock.

Zack looked down at the stone itself, no more than an inch thick. He wiped away the dust and dirt on the back, and soon saw that it was carved with a series of runic symbols. The other two treasures had simply been marked with a single word: *Faith* and *Courage*. The stone, however, was inscribed with several lines. Without Yggdrasil's Key, Zack knew that the symbols would look like a random series of straight and diagonal lines. With the key, he was able to read them as if they were plain English.

> For any quest there is a price.
> The time has come for Sacrifice.
> What fate has brought, so it will be.
> Now use this stone,
> Destroy the key.

CHAPTER TWELVE

Zack had come to accept that he would one day have to give up the key. Maybe to Jok, or to the Free Man. But he hadn't ever thought it would be destroyed, or that it even *could* be destroyed. And now that was exactly what he was supposed to do.

Now was the time to open the third chamber while he still could. It wasn't even clear yet if there would be a third treasure, but unlocking the chest would leave his options open.

He carried the heavy stone to the center of the courtyard and set it down next to the chest. The third chamber was marked *Sacrifice* in the same runic symbols as the stone. Zack fit one of the key's three stems into the third lock and opened it.

A crude rendering of Asgard's towers was carved on the underside of the lid. Zack knew that he was looking at one-third of a larger map, showing where the treasures had been hidden. The rest of the map was inside the other two lids, now permanently sealed shut.

It had all come to this. He looked down at the key, perhaps for the last time.

Hang on a second. . . .

Two things occurred to Zack.

If he smashed the key, how was he going to get home again?

But if he didn't do it, and didn't finish the quest, was it actually possible he would never be born?

Either way, he was giving something up.

That's why it's called Sacrifice.

Images of home passed through his mind. He saw Ollie sitting on the front stoop, waiting for him to come back that night in the rain. He saw his father, making pancake sandwiches at the kitchen stove. He saw Ashley, trying to open her stubborn locker. In his mind, they all looked back, watching his every move, waiting for him to decide.

But given the choice between never getting home and never being born, he knew what he had to do. The truth of it settled in his stomach like a pancake sandwich made of concrete.

He had to destroy Yggdrasil's Key.

With shaking hands, he laid the key on the ground. Then he picked up the heavy stone by its edges and hefted it up to shoulder level. Jok called out from the gate, but without the key in his hand, Zack couldn't understand what he was saying. It didn't matter anyway. He spread his feet wide and heaved the stone high above his head.

Jok bellowed at him, and Zack shut his eyes.

This is it.

A bolt of energy ran up his legs, through his body, and into his raised arms. Zack felt his strength focused into one task, as he had never felt it before. He opened his eyes and brought the stone down as hard as he could.

A geyser of white light broke free and shot straight up from the key. A muffled boom came from beneath it, like an underground explosion. The earth seemed to eject Zack from where he stood, and he flew backward through the air.

He landed, softly somehow. When he opened his eyes, he was on his back, staring straight up. Pale yellow rings of light passed over him, like ripples in a pond. He looked over and saw the key in pieces on the ground nearby. The light pulsed up and away from that spot with an electric throbbing sound. Zack could feel his skin prickle as the rings passed through him.

Slowly, the pulsing subsided. The rings of light grew faint, then disappeared. Zack went and stood over the key. It was in four cleanly broken parts—three stems and the round centerpiece, with its swirl of carved branches and leaves still intact. He bent to pick them up. The moment his hand touched metal, all of the shouting from the gate came clear again and his heart soared.

"Zack!"

"Lost Boy, what's happening?"

He squeezed the pieces in his hand. The key's power was still with him.

Jok's voice came above the others. "Quiet!" He pointed to where a pair of tall bejeweled doors on the courtyard had opened. And standing there, looking at Zack, was the Free Man.

It was him but it wasn't him. He was taller than before, taller than Zack and Jok, a larger version of himself. His plain tunic and wool pants were gone. Now he wore the rich robes of Asgard. A gold coil, sculpted like a snake, wound around his left arm. He walked calmly toward Zack.

"I *knew* you had something else going on!" Zack shouted. The Free Man didn't even crack a smile, but Zack couldn't help his excitement. He shook the Free Man's hand much harder than he meant to.

"Okay, please tell me you're going to give me some answers here," he said.

The Free Man took his time. He looked at the pieces of the key in Zack's hand. "Keep the center amulet, and put the other pieces in the chest," he said.

Zack held up the round metal piece. He almost didn't want to ask his question. "Can this thing still . . ."

"Take you home?" the Free Man said. "When the time is right, yes."

Zack breathed once deeply. As he exhaled, it was as if a heavy weight left him. He felt physically lighter.

He looked back at the gates, where everyone had gone down onto one knee. They watched silently, helmets in hand.

"What about everyone else?" Zack asked. It didn't seem fair to do this alone. But the Free Man only motioned toward the chest.

The amulet, as the Free Man had called it, slipped easily into Zack's pocket. Then Zack went obediently and placed the three remaining pieces in the empty chamber. As soon as he did, the chest filled with more of the same golden light as it had twice before, with the first two treasures. The light flowed like water up and over the top of the chamber. Then the lid slowly pulled closed on its own. With a soft hiss, the lock fused over, and the chest grew still.

Zack waited to see if there was something more. When nothing happened, he burst out, "Can they all come in now?"

"No," the Free Man said plainly, "but you may go see them." He motioned toward the gate and Zack took off.

The entrance swung open just wide enough to let Zack pass. Everyone was still down on one knee. He saw exactly what they were about to do. They were about to start calling out "Hail, Lost Boy!" They had done it before, and it was always embarrassing.

Instead, he cut them off. He remembered something he had showed them once or twice. Something his father had taught him a long time ago. The Minnesota fight song. He put both fists into the air, and shouted out, "V – I – K – I – N – G – S!"

Everyone leapt to their feet. "Go, Vikings, let's go!"

The solemn mood shattered, and everyone slammed in toward Zack, with a torrent of cheering and hugging and congratulating. Jok reached him first. He lifted Zack up in the air with one clean motion and, as the rest of the tribe closed in, landed him on all of their shoulders.

Harald started to chant, "Lost! Boy! Lost! Boy! Lost! Boy!" and everyone else joined in.

Someone tossed Olaf up as well. He and Zack pointed and laughed at each other as the tribe bounced them from one set of hands to another.

"Is good to be done with the quest!" Olaf shouted. "Is time for feasting and all!"

Zack's relief and happiness and exhaustion washed together into a new sense of well-being. He reached out and patted people on the shoulder, and knocked Sven playfully upside the head as he surfed the crowd. He even high-fived Valdis as he passed over her head.

It was Sigurd who finally set him down, his knees nearly buckling under Zack's weight. Zack looked at him and wondered how he'd ever thought any of Jok's tribe could have been working as a spy for Erik. He reached out and shook Sigurd's hand. Sigurd opened his mouth as if he were about to speak. Then he let out a huge burp and nudged Zack back into the crowd.

Hilda collared him next. "Helga and I are proud to have fought for you, Lost Boy. You are always welcome in Konur."

Zack shook their hands as well. "And you guys are welcome in Minneapolis."

Both twins looked puzzled, but already Zack was pushed along. Lars, Harald, and Sven all closed around him. They stepped in all at once, with a group belly bump that knocked the wind out of Zack's lungs.

"So the quest is done," Jok said. He paused, and the noise of the group began to die down. "But what is next? Zack, were you shown the purpose of this quest?"

Murmurs began to travel around the tribe, and the same question occurred to Zack. He'd been so focused on the idea that completing the quest was the only way to save his own life, but everyone else must be waiting for some kind of treasure. And shouldn't they get that?

Zack saw the Free Man standing near at the gate. He held up a hand, and the crowd grew quiet.

"Jok, Valdis, Zack," he said. "Please follow me."

The three of them looked at one another. Jok stepped forward first, and they followed the Free Man back through the gates, which clanged shut, leaving the others outside.

"What happens now?" Harald called after them. "Free Man! What do we have now that the quest is over?"

The Free Man paused and turned back to them. "Your glory is assured," he said. Then he motioned toward Jok. "As to the rest, your chieftain will bring you news when we are through."

Zack heard a few frustrated groans, but mostly the tribe still laughed and cheered.

"I could use a gold sword!" called Sven.

"Jok, don't forget a barrel of Odin's finest!" yelled Lars.

"Is good to see Zack again!" Olaf called out. Zack looked over his shoulder and flashed a thumbs-up. There was definitely going to be some major feasting back in Lykill.

The Free Man went to the middle of the courtyard and picked up Yggdrasil's Chest as if it weighed nothing. Then Jok, Valdis, and Zack followed him inside.

They passed into a long corridor, but it was like entering

a dense forest. Vines covered the walls. Trees lined the passage like columns, holding up the ceiling. Their roots grew right through the polished marble floor. "Mind your step," the Free Man said, just before Zack stumbled over one of them.

Jok walked between Valdis and Zack, with his arms around their shoulders. All three stared with open mouths as the passage gave way to a huge room.

A breeze blew over them as they stepped inside. The walls were natural rock, as craggy and as high as the cliff Zack had climbed several days before. The ceiling, far overhead, was painted to depict a dark stormy sky. As Zack watched, the gray clouds came to life, passing slowly across the scene. A flash of lightning appeared, followed by a low rumble of thunder and a brief rain shower that moved through the room. When Zack looked up again, the ceiling had turned a bright sky blue.

"Where are we?" he asked quietly. Jok nudged him and pointed to the far wall, where an enormous sculpture was carved into the rock. It showed a muscular, bearded figure driving a chariot, pulled by two great horned rams. The figure held a short-handled hammer over his head.

"This is Thor's temple," said the Free Man.

The sculpture was familiar. "That was Thor outside, wasn't it?" Zack said. "Up on the walkway. The big, grumpy-looking guy with the red hair."

Another roll of thunder echoed around them.

Jok bowed his head. "Are we worthy of being here?"

"You are worthy," the Free Man said. He carried Yggdrasil's Chest to the far end of the room and placed it on a plain stone pedestal. "And you are ready to hear what I have to tell you."

He motioned them closer, then went on. "I am not the Free Man, as you know me. I am not of Midgard, and I am not human. I am Modi."

Jok and Valdis immediately went down again onto one knee.

"It is all right," he said. "Please stand."

Zack looked from Jok to the Free Man and back again. Jok answered his unspoken question. "Modi is the son of Thor," he said.

Zack looked back at the Free Man again, mentally running through everything he thought he knew about him. "So I guess that explains the whole ice cabin, and the talking to animals. Although, I have to say, your cooking wasn't exactly . . ." He trailed off when he realized they were all just staring at him.

"Just a joke," he said quietly. "Sorry. Go on."

"I have many things to tell you," Modi said, "and not much time." He clasped his hands under his chin, composing his thoughts.

Finally, he looked up at Zack. "The quest began here, in this room. It was conceived by Thor himself, as a test of your worthiness. A test which you have passed."

"Why was there a test at all?" Zack said. It was hard to ask just one question at a time, he had so many.

Modi held up a finger. "I am speaking out of order. There is one more thing you need to know first." Again, he paused, then turned to Jok and Valdis. "I once knew a woman. A human. Over time, our love grew, and eventually, we had a son. While I am of the Aesir family of gods, this son was born a mortal human. He aged normally, as humans do, and as his mother would have done if she had lived."

"Is the boy still living?" Jok asked.

Modi looked straight at him. "Jok, that son was you."

Jok's eyes widened and he stood very still, then took Valdis's hand.

Zack stared at them. It felt as though his brain was running out of room. The first thought that came to mind popped out of his mouth. "How old are you?"

"I'm much, much older than I look," Modi said.

"But . . ." Zack went on, trying make sense of it. "You guys don't look anything alike."

Modi nodded. "That's true. Jok looks much more like his grandfather."

"Thor," Valdis said quietly. "Of course." She reached up and put a hand to Jok's face, then looked up at the giant sculpture on the wall.

"I had always thought I was an orphan," Jok said evenly. "And now you say I am—" He looked down at Valdis. "That we are part of Thor's bloodline?"

"This knowledge is what the quest has brought you," Modi said.

Jok nodded quietly, taking it in with an amazing calm.

"Your mother, Thasil, died when you were born," Modi told him. "When it became clear you were fully human, Thor refused to allow you shelter here in Asgard. Instead, you were left as a foundling in Lykill."

Zack breathed in and out slowly. It seemed Asgard could be just as harsh a place as the rest of this world.

Modi went on. "Thor commanded that a test for this new human lineage be created. The Prophecy was set forth. Yggdrasil's Chest and Key were created. The three treasures were forged here and then scattered throughout the worlds.

"Jok, you are the first of Thor's human bloodline, but it was not enough that you be tested. My father insisted that the lineage prove worthy as well." He turned slowly and looked at Zack.

"Wait a second," Zack said. "What do you mean?"

The Free Man gave Zack one of his I-think-you-know-what-I-mean looks.

Zack spoke slowly. It was too much to get out all at once. "So, Jok . . . and you . . ."

"And Thor himself," Jok prompted.

"You're all my . . . I'm your . . ." Zack swallowed once. "We're related? I'm Thor's great-great-great . . . something . . . grandson?"

"Like your father, and your father's father," Modi told him.

"My father?" Zack shouted. It followed logically, but he hadn't even gotten there yet. He looked at Jok's face and saw the similarity to Jock Gilman in a whole new way.

Zack had begun to feel smothered by all the new information. Now, suddenly, it felt as though his mind had squeezed tightly closed and was opening back up again. Everything he knew about himself—and his father—was expanding.

"I came through time to bring you the key," Modi said. "The tests, of faith, and courage, and sacrifice, were yours to accept or refuse. I can now tell you that if you had refused them, or failed, the lineage would have been struck from history."

"And now . . ." Zack could practically hear the *click, click, click* of all the pieces falling into place. "Now I . . . get to be born? Now that I finished this?"

"That is why the Prophecy viewed you as an orphan. Until now," Modi said. Then he turned back to Jok and Valdis.

"Valdis, your vein of our lineage has many great things before it. I will not tell you what waits, but you will be a great leader, like your father."

Valdis smiled appreciatively and looked at the floor. Zack had never seen her so humble.

"And Jok," Modi said. "Your son will have a son, who will have a son, who will have a son, and it will go on to Zack's generation and beyond."

"Son?" Jok asked, confused. "But I have no son."

"You will."

Jok ran a hand through his beard. "What do you mean?"

"You were tested in a different way. Thor demands great

152

faith and courage and sacrifice of his lineage—not just on the battlefield, but in acts of love as well."

Jok sat on a stone bench and looked at the ground, still listening. Modi sat down next to him and put a hand on his shoulder. "Jok, throughout this quest, there is one thing above all that you have never lost hope of finding."

Zack was shocked to see a tear roll down Jok's cheek.

A door at the far end of the temple opened, and a woman ran out, straight into Jok's arms. Valdis let out a cry and wrapped her arms around both of them.

Zack barely caught a glimpse of the woman before her face was buried in Jok's shoulder.

Winniferd.

It was Jok's wife. And her face was exactly that of Zack's own mother.

Zack stared at Winniferd's back, and everything else dropped away. Memories of his mother flooded in. He felt tears running down his own cheeks.

"Winniferd was taken and held here safely until the quest was completed. It was Thor's bidding," Modi told them.

Jok and Winniferd pulled apart, both of their faces streaked with tears. Winniferd took Valdis's chin in her hands and then hugged her tightly again.

"We can never have back the nine years taken from us," Jok said.

"I know," Modi said. "The alternative was to end your life before it even began. And that I could not bear to do."

Zack barely heard what they were saying. All he felt was

an old pain, more intense than it had been in years—the knowledge that his mother was gone forever. He knew in his heart and his gut that there would be no happy reunion like this for him. A spark of jealousy rose up, but it ebbed away the moment Winniferd turned and spoke to him.

"Is this the Lost Boy?" she asked. Her voice was like another old memory come to life.

Zack tried to say hello, but choked on his own words.

"This is Zack," Jok said. "Without him, we could not have gotten here."

"I must tell you one more thing," Modi said. "Today is an ending and a beginning. The glory of the quest is not riches, but simply that you will carry on Thor's great bloodline."

"There is no greater glory than that," Jok said happily.

"Your worldly troubles may be just as many as before," Modi continued. "Erik the Horrible may or may not find his way back to Midgard. But what I am telling you is this, Jok: Continue as the great leader you have been. Carry on the bloodline. There are more great leaders to come." Everyone turned and looked at Zack.

Zack blushed deeply and shoved his hands into his pockets.

"Yeah," he said, looking at the floor. "Great leader. Right."

But he couldn't help smiling.

CHAPTER THIRTEEN

"So what happens now?" Zack asked.

Jok, Valdis, and Winniferd stood off to the side. Valdis's head lay against her mother's shoulder, and the three of them spoke to one another in soft tones.

"Your life goes on," Modi answered.

"That's it?" Zack asked. "Just like that?"

"That depends on what you make of all this. Your life has not changed, Zack. Remember that. Everything is as you left it."

Zack saw his house and his living room in his mind. The torn cardboard goalpost hanging on the wall. The empty soda cans piled up next to the kitchen garbage. His father. His sister.

"So everything just goes back to normal after all this?" he said.

"Not exactly," Modi answered. "One thing will have changed."

"What?"

"The only thing that really can change."

"What are you talking about?"

Modi gave Zack a familiar look, the one he always gave instead of a straight answer.

Zack thought for a minute. Then he rolled his eyes. "Me, right? I'm the thing that changed. That's it, huh? Kind of corny for someone as deep as you, Free Man—I mean, Modi."

"Change is not a gift to be underestimated," Modi said. "Don't squander it. If you can change the way you see things, Zack, you can do anything."

"Sounds like something my dad would say."

A light snow began to fall. Zack smiled up at the ceiling, which was now silvery gray. "This place is amazing."

"You still have the amulet?" Modi asked him.

Zack reached into his pocket and held up the round metal piece. "Can I keep this? As a souvenir?"

Modi nodded. "It will take you home."

"I just want to say good-bye to everyone first."

He turned to the spot where Jok, Winniferd, and Valdis had been standing a moment ago—but they were gone.

"Hey, where'd they go?"

Zack turned back again, and Modi had disappeared as well. The snow was falling harder. It began to collect around his feet.

"Modi?"

The doors of the temple flew open and a full blizzard raced in like a freight train. Zack covered his face with his arms and clutched the amulet as it began to heat up in his hand.

"Wait! I'm not ready! I don't—"

Another howl of wind stole the end of his sentence. Suddenly he was in the midst of a storm. The only thing he could see was Yggdrasil's Chest, still within reach but barely visible. The wind gusted and blew him off balance. Zack leaned on the chest for support. He shielded his eyes against the bits of ice that stung his skin. The key grew steadily warmer until he had to hold it with the edge of his sleeve.

It was happening too fast. How could he just leave like that?

Not that he had a choice.

The chest gave way. Suddenly he wasn't leaning on it anymore. He squinted down through the blowing snow. Dark wood and iron faded to pale gray. Within moments, the chest dissolved into dust, and the dust was absorbed into the storm.

He stumbled away, lifting his feet from the drifts around his knees. His limbs were stiff. The temperature was still falling fast.

He hadn't gone far when a loud honking caught his attention. A huge snowplow emerged from the whiteness and bore down on him. Zack jumped out of the way just in time. He rolled over in the snow and saw the plow's red taillights moving up the street.

He was in the middle of the road. A row of nearby hedges came into view. And beyond that, he saw the vague outline of his own house. That was when he realized the amulet in his hand had gone cold again. The burnished silver had turned back to rust, but the carved leaves and branches were still recognizable. He pocketed it, and headed up the driveway.

Jock was standing near the front door with his coat on.

"Dad!"

Zack heard the excitement in his own voice. He knew it would seem odd, but he couldn't help himself. As far as his father knew, Zack had never left. Coming back was always one of the strangest parts.

"I was just coming to get you," Jock said. "What was that all about?"

Everything was the same as before. The fire in the hearth was still blazing, maybe even still burning up the last of Zack's maps and charts—things, he realized, he wouldn't need anymore. He looked around the room, smiling.

"What a freak." Valerie stood by the fire, looking at him like he was crazy.

Jock took off his coat and tossed it on the couch. "I'm glad you weren't out there too long. A storm like this can be dangerous."

Zack stared at his father. He really did look like Thor.

"Yeah," he said finally. "I'm all set."

"What happened to your arm?"

Zack looked down and saw a long tear in his sleeve. A line of dried blood showed where Erik had cut him.

"Uh . . . I got cut."

"Well, I can see that," Jock said. "Come here. Let's get you fixed up."

Zack followed him to the bathroom. He continued to stare at his father's face as Jock washed and bandaged his arm.

"Are you all right?" Jock asked him. "You look kind of funny."

"Yeah," he said, as normally as he could muster. His mind raced.

"Good."

Zack reached into his pocket. "In fact, here. I want to give you something for the game this weekend. Something for the Vikings." He held out the old rusted amulet for Jock. "I know it doesn't look like much, but it's good luck. Really."

Jock smiled down at it without touching it.

"So it's done, then," he said.

The words sent a chill down Zack's spine. Could it be a coincidence? Did Jock know what he was saying?

"What do you mean?"

"The quest. You've finished it."

Zack's chills turned to goose bumps.

His father's eyes misted over. To Zack's utter amazement, Jock reached out, enclosed him in a tight embrace, and said, "I knew it. I knew you could do it."

Wait. What? Wait. Huh?

"How do you . . . What . . . How . . ." Zack began several sentences at once. Finally, he said. "How do you know that?"

"Why do you think I'm such a Vikings fan?" Jock asked.

Zack sat down hard on the toilet seat and looked at the amulet. "I thought—"

"I know," Jock said. "It's a lot to take in all at once. Come here. I want to show you something."

Jock led Zack back to his bedroom. He opened a drawer

and pulled out a small wooden box. Inside was another round amulet. Its size and shape were similar to Zack's, but the design was different. Zack saw a serpent's head worked in among the interlocked strands of rusted metal. He could barely take his eyes away from it.

"So . . . you've done this, too?" he asked.

"Yep. And your grandfather, too. Every generation."

"Why didn't you ever say anything? I thought I was totally on my own."

"That's the idea," Jock said. "It's a lone quest. You had to make the decisions by yourself. That's the way it works."

"And you've known all along?"

Jock nodded. His face was still beaming with pride. "Are you kidding? You've been like a zombie around here. It was kind of hard to miss it."

Zack looked at the two amulets. "Modi told me I was the only one—"

"The only one to use that key," Jock said. "It's different for everyone."

"The key?" Zack asked.

Jock nodded. "The key, the quest, the tests. All of it."

Zack smiled up at Jock, feeling half crazy, half relieved. "What about you? What was your quest like?"

Jock tilted back his head and roared with laughter. He collared Zack and squeezed him around the neck. "Well, that's a good story. How much time do you have?"

CHAPTER FOURTEEN

Zack caught Ollie up on everything as they walked to school the next day. They passed huge drifts where the snowplows had pushed away the storm.

"So what do you think?" Ollie asked. "Are you ready for twenty-first-century life full-time?"

"I'm ready for twenty-first-century *food* full-time, that's for sure," Zack said. Even Jock had been surprised at how much breakfast Zack put away that morning.

"How about twenty-first-century girls?" Ollie said. "Are you going to have an actual conversation with Ashley once and for all?"

Zack shrugged. The image of Asleif falling into the void still haunted him. "I don't know," he said. "I already got burned once. Besides, Eric gave her playoff tickets. She's supposed to bring a friend and go with him and Doug Horner to the game. I'm not going to get into some kind of competition. Not with Spangler. Forget it."

"Come on," Ollie said. "You used Spangler to rearrange the library. You're the Lost Boy!" He reached out and tried to push Zack off the sidewalk.

Zack hip-checked him and Ollie flopped into the snow. "Yeah," he said. "I'm the Lost Boy." It was easier to play along than to admit that he had no intention of talking to Ashley.

So when Ashley walked right up to him at his locker that morning, Zack could not have been more surprised. The hard part was not showing it.

Easy, Gilman. Easy, easy.

"What's up?" she said.

Zack's stomach fluttered. "Uh, hi," he said.

Not so casual.

"How's it going?" he added, a bit more brightly.

Zack had always been tongue-tied around Ashley. Now it was as if there was a third person standing there, whispering in his ear and distracting him from his already muddled thoughts.

Can you trust her? Do you even know who she is?

"Listen," she said. "This is kind of a weird question, but do you like football?"

"I guess," Zack said. "A little more than I used to, at least."

"'Cause someone gave me two tickets for the playoffs this weekend—"

A cold awareness gripped Zack.

Stop. Don't go any further.

"—and I'm supposed to bring a friend—"

She was actually inviting him on the double date that Eric Spangler had envisioned for himself and Doug Horner.

"—and I just thought you might be interested."

Zack was stunned.

No way, no way, no way.

He knew he had to say something right away, or look like an idiot.

How was he going to say no to Ashley? Everything had gotten out of hand all over again.

And then, all of a sudden, Zack was opening his mouth and saying . . .

"Sounds great."

The only reason to say no was because he was afraid of what might happen. And that was no reason at all. Not anymore.

His instinct had gotten there before he did, but it seemed clear now. He felt his shoulders go down an inch or two. His throat didn't feel like it was about to close up anymore, either.

Ashley flashed him another smile. "They're good seats, too," she said. "Fifty-yard line, if you care about that kind of thing."

"Well, not really," Zack said, and a new idea started forming in his head. "But I know someone who does."

❧

They all rode to the Metrodome in the Gilmans' Winnebago, known as the Winnie in Jock's circle. Everyone was in extra-high spirits. Zack had used his original ticket to invite Ollie, who reluctantly agreed to come along. Ashley gladly traded her fifty-yard-line seats with Jock and Swan so that she, Zack, and Ollie could all sit together up in the nosebleeder section.

"I think I'm supposed to meet someone at those seats,"

Ashley said. "So if anyone's looking for me, just tell them where I am."

Jock turned back from the driver's seat and grinned. His white teeth stood out from his purple-painted face. "Ashley, we only just met you, but already I think we love you."

Swan howled out in agreement and pounded the ceiling of the Winnie with his fists.

Zack watched Jock, bouncing from side to side while he drove, like a kid who couldn't wait to get where he was going.

"Hey, Zack!" Jock called to him. "Who's it gonna be today, huh?"

"It's funny," Zack yelled back. "But I've got this weird feeling the Bears are going down!" The two of them howled with laughter while Ashley gave them both a puzzled look.

At the Metrodome, the parking lot was crawling with fans. Zack, Ashley, and Ollie crowded in toward the turnstiles. As usual, Zack was a head above most of the people around him. When they got closer, he saw Eric and Doug, in their orange-and-blue Chicago jackets. They were headed for the same entrance. Eric glanced over, and for a brief moment, their eyes locked. A flash of panic crossed Eric's features. It was the same expression Zack had seen on his face just before Yggdrasil's Key had tossed him across the school library.

Eric looked away first. He pulled on Doug's sleeve and said something Zack couldn't hear. Doug seemed confused, but a moment later, the two of them stepped out of line and headed for a different entrance.

"What's that smile about?" Ashley asked, glancing up at him.

"Nothing," Zack said. "I just saw some people I know."

✤

The Winnie nearly rocked off its wheels as it headed home that evening.

Final score, Vikings 31, Bears 7.

"And they only scored it on a bad call!" hooted Swan, to the screaming approval of everyone around him.

The noise more than filled the small RV, but for once, Zack didn't mind. He was pressed between Ollie and Ashley on the bench seat in the back. It wasn't exactly a date, but it was more of one than Eric Spangler had gotten that day.

Jock sat in the driver's seat up front, his voice clear above everyone else's.

"We're going to the Super Bowl!" he howled, for the fifth time in as many minutes.

Harlan, Larry, Smitty, and Swan belly-bumped in the middle of the Winnie and fell back in four directions, spilling their sodas and crashing into everything in sight.

"Your father and his friends are hilarious!" Ashley shouted in his ear.

Zack nodded. "They're weird, but they're harmless!"

He watched the dark road recede out the Winnie's back window, and an old but unfamiliar feeling crept over him. For the first time he could remember in a long while, Zack was exactly where he wanted to be.

"Hey, Jock!" yelled Larry. "Turn up the music!"

The Minnesota fight song blared over the Winnie's stereo. As it wound up for a big finish, Zack jumped to his feet and joined with the others, singing at the top of his lungs.

"V – I – K – I – N – G – S! Go, Vikings, let's go!"